Welcome to February's ~~~
from Harlequin Presen~~~

Be sure not to miss the ~~~
series THE ROYAL HOU~~~ will the beautiful
island of Niroli finally be able to crown the true
heir to the throne? Find out in *A Royal Bride at the Sheikh's Command* by favorite author Penny Jordan!
Plus, continuing her trilogy about three passionate and brooding men, THE RICH, THE RUTHLESS AND THE REALLY HANDSOME, Lynne Graham brings you *The Greek Tycoon's Defiant Bride*, where Leonidas is determined to take the mother of his son as his wife!

Also this month…can a billionaire ever change his bad-boy ways? Discover the answer in Miranda Lee's *The Guardian's Forbidden Mistress!* Susan Stephens brings you *Bought: One Island, One Bride*, where a Greek tycoon seduces a feisty beauty, then buys her body and soul. In *The Sicilian's Virgin Bride* by Sarah Morgan, Rocco Castellani tracks down his estranged wife—and will finally claim his virgin bride! In *Expecting His Love-Child*, Carol Marinelli tells the story of Millie, who is hiding a secret—she's pregnant with Levander's baby! In *The Billionaire's Marriage Mission* by Helen Brooks, it looks like wealthy Travis Black won't get what he wants for once—or will he? Finally, new author Christina Hollis brings you an innocent virgin who must give herself to an Italian tycoon for one night of unsurpassable passion, in her brilliant debut novel *One Night in his Bed*. Happy reading!

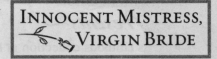

INNOCENT MISTRESS, VIRGIN BRIDE

Wedded and bedded for the very first time

Classic romances from your favorite
Presents authors

Available this month:

One Night in His Bed
by Christina Hollis

Available only from Harlequin Presents®

Don

Christina Hollis

ONE NIGHT IN HIS BED

INNOCENT MISTRESS,
VIRGIN BRIDE

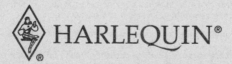

HARLEQUIN®

TORONTO • NEW YORK • LONDON
AMSTERDAM • PARIS • SYDNEY • HAMBURG
STOCKHOLM • ATHENS • TOKYO • MILAN • MADRID
PRAGUE • WARSAW • BUDAPEST • AUCKLAND

ISBN-13: 978-0-373-12706-1
ISBN-10:   0-373-12706-5

ONE NIGHT IN HIS BED

First North American Publication 2008.

www.eHarlequin.com

Printed in U.S.A.

All about the author…
Christina Hollis

CHRISTINA HOLLIS was born a few miles from Bath, England. She began writing as soon as she could hold a pencil, but was always told to concentrate on getting a "proper" job.

She joined a financial institution straight from school. After some years of bean counting, report writing and partying hard, she reached the heady heights of "gofer" in the marketing department. At that point, a wonderful case of love at first sight led to marriage within months. She was still spending all her spare time writing, and when one of her plays was short-listed in a BBC competition, her husband suggested she try writing full-time.

Half a dozen full-length novels and a lot of nonfiction work for national magazines followed. After a long maternity break, she joined a creative writing course to update her skills. There, she was encouraged to experiment with a form she loved to read but had never tried writing before—romance fiction. Her first romance, *The Italian Billionaire's Virgin,* began life as a two-thousand-word college assignment. She thinks that writing romance must be the best job in the world! It gives her the chance to do something she loves while hopefully bringing pleasure to others.

Christina has two lovely children and a cat. She lives on the Welsh border and enjoys reading, gardening and feeding the birds. Visit her Web site at www.christinahollis.com.

To Jenny, whose enthusiasm
really keeps me going!

CHAPTER ONE

'SUPERSTITIOUS old Enrica saw a black cat this morning. She told me it means there are pirates in town. You had better put on something sexier than that black shroud and try to catch yourself a rich one, Sienna!' Imelda Basso jeered out of an upstairs window. Down in the courtyard, her stepdaughter Sienna gritted her teeth and smiled. She said nothing. Sometimes, silence was her only weapon against Imelda.

Sienna loaded a last box into the local Co-operative's van and escaped to market. Working on the stall got her out of the house, but freedom was a mixed blessing. It made her feel like a hen released from a broody coop. The noise and dazzling colour of Portofino always came as a shock to her. It was such a contrast with her daily life that all Sienna wanted to do when she got there was to retreat back into herself, to concentrate on her knitting and take up as little space as possible. But that was no good. Nobody would buy from a mouse. The Piccia Co-operative needed sales. Its members relied on this stall. They intended to increase their contribution to local charities this year, too. That meant everyone had to do their bit—Sienna included. She had to push herself.

She was developing a coping strategy. She kept her head down, and made sure she always looked busy. It was the perfect way to avoid having to talk to anybody until the exact moment they were ready to buy.

Sienna recognised a lot of familiar faces around the market, although she had never been brave enough to strike up a conversation with any of them. Yet today was different. Someone new caught her eye—and held it. A tall stranger was moving through the chaos of deliveries and conversations on the other side of the square. Sienna had to look away, fast. He was so different from the market men that her stomach contracted. A single glance was enough to tell her that this was someone special. He was really well dressed, and the quiet confidence of his movements set him apart from the brash, swaggering pitchers around him. Sienna risked a couple of direct looks at the stranger, as well as more covert glances from beneath her lashes. She reassured herself that no one would suspect a shy widow of anything more than curiosity.

The new arrival was certainly worth examining. His determined attitude, coupled with that neat dark hair and the clean, strong lines of his jaw, marked him out as someone very special indeed. He moved from stall to stall with all the style of a Roman emperor on a tour of inspection. Sienna wondered what it was like to be so self-assured. This man obviously expected to go anywhere and do anything. She watched as he sampled olives, tasted walnuts, or accepted a spoonful of goats' cheese spread on a biscuit. He did not stop anywhere long enough to buy, but moved on in a restless search for the next novelty. Sienna would never have dared to try something at a stall and then leave without purchasing. She wondered how he could have the nerve. His easy manner showed it was not a problem for him,

Hypnotised by watching him idle along from place to place, she suddenly realised it was almost time for her stall to come under his scrutiny. Her mind dissolved in horror. What would she say? Here was a gorgeous man—with plenty of money to spend, judging by his appearance. He would be an ideal customer. If only she could succeed in getting him to buy where everyone else in the market had failed…

With difficulty, she kept her gaze away from the approaching stranger. If she didn't look at him directly, he might pass on by. She screwed her hands into balls of nerves. Why did this have to happen when she was working alone? Anna Maria or any one of the other co-op members would have leapt forward and made a sale. All Sienna could do was blush and shrink and turn aside, hoping that the handsome newcomer would pass straight by.

She counted the change in the pouch at her waist. Then she switched her attention back to her table, making sure the goods were still neatly displayed, touching everything as though for luck. She repeated her little rituals until she was sure he must have passed by. Even so, it was quite a while before she felt brave enough to glance around the market again.

There was no sign of the stranger. With a huge sigh of relief Sienna relaxed. It was all too much for her. She hadn't wanted to be seen blushing, as she knew she would have done if she'd spoken to the handsome stranger. In Piccia, where she lived, good reputations took a lifetime to forge. And people expected to see a certain standard of behaviour from a widow. One word or action out of place could destroy her reputation in an instant. Sienna thought of the local woman whose husband had divorced her in order to marry his mistress. The wife had been the innocent party, but looks and whispers had followed her everywhere. Eventually she had been hounded out of her birthplace.

Sienna could not bear to think of being the subject of gossip. Her stepmother, Imelda, would never forgive her. And her anger frightened Sienna. Just the thought of Imelda's displeasure was enough to keep Sienna on the straight and narrow—but then virtue was an easy path in Piccia. There was no temptation. All the boys left as soon as they could. Only men with private incomes or those too old to escape lived in Piccia now.

Sienna sighed. She liked the quiet village life, but it came at a huge price. Imelda was determined to marry her off to a rich man again as soon as it was decent. Sienna's late husband had had only one blood relative, a distant cousin called Claudio di Imperia, and Imelda had him in mind as Sienna's next suitor. One look at Claudio's pinched, pale face had told Sienna that 'fun' was not a word with any meaning for him. If I have to be married, why can't *I* choose who it's going to be? she thought angrily.

The good-looking stranger was now bending over a stand on the far side of the market. He was concentrating on a display of everything imaginable that could be made from chestnuts. While he was busy, Sienna took the chance to study him again—but only while the other stallholders weren't looking.

The visitor was dressed in Armani, she noticed, and his thick dark hair was neatly trimmed. What a contrast he made with her unwanted future husband. Claudio wore his frayed cuffs and bad haircut like medals for economy. But Imelda always said it didn't matter what a man looked like as long as he had plenty of money in the bank. In Sienna's house, Imelda Basso's word was law. The only thing *that* woman feared was public opinion—which was why Sienna was determined to wear black for as long as possible. It was protection. No one in the village would forgive Imelda if she tried to marry off her stepdaughter when the 'poor girl' was still in mourning.

Snared away from her thoughts, Sienna realised in a panic that he was coming in her direction again. She looked down quickly, already worrying about what to say if he spoke to her. Then she remembered her stepmother's mocking laughter. *Who is going to be interested in Piccia's homespun rubbish?*

Sienna's shoulders sagged. Was there no escape from the echo of that woman's voice? It was even invading her daydreams.

Was Imelda right? Would anybody as rich as him be interested in her stall? The gorgeous stranger would probably buy some of those dark handmade chocolates wrapped in crackling cellophane and ribbon for his equally shrink-wrapped and sophisticated girlfriend. He's bound to have one, Sienna thought, and I'll bet *she* never wears black.

'Excuse me, miss—I wonder if you could direct me to the Church of San Gregorio?'

A loud, cultured voice made her flush with confusion. She looked up—but it was not the person she had hoped it would be. Instead of her dashing hero, she found herself staring at the expectant faces of a couple of tourists.

All Sienna's tension dissolved in a self-conscious giggle. She gave the directions, and even managed to exchange a few cheerful words. Then a cloud blotted out her relief. While she had been busy chatting, a presence had arrived beside her. That was the only way she could describe it. The tall, well-dressed stranger had materialised at her elbow.

All her worries flooded back, stifling her voice as soon as the tourists said goodbye. She was alone with him. Sienna had no option but to look up and smile. Straight away she made sure she could not be accused of flirting. It didn't matter that she was twenty kilometres from home, Sienna knew that the moment she showed the slightest interest in any male over the age of ten, the news would reach her stepmother before you could say 'torrid affair'.

The vision smiled back. Sienna gazed at him, at a loss. And then he spoke.

'I heard you speaking English to that couple.' He came straight to the point in a distinctive accent. It matched his frank, typically American expression. 'I wonder—could you please direct me to the best restaurant around here?'

Was that all he needed? Sienna wanted to feel relief rush through her, but it didn't happen. His steady gaze was too intense for that. His dark brown eyes mesmerised her, in the split second she allowed herself to look up into his face. Quickly, she looked down again. The very *best* place to eat was about twenty kilometres away, up in the hills. No one in Piccia could afford to eat in Il Pettirosso, where Anna Maria's husband Angelo worked, but it was the restaurant Sienna always visited in her daydreams. As all the staff were local, and this visitor had chosen her for her ability to speak English, it might not be for him. But his confident yet relaxed stance told Sienna that this man would fit in anywhere. And he is exactly the sort who might try and turn my simplest reply into a conversation, she thought nervously.

Conversation was a risk Sienna could not take. She had enough grief in her life already, and didn't want any more. This would never have happened if the man had bought something when he'd first walked into the market, she reflected. The other stallholders always spoke English when a customer showed real signs of spending money. She glanced sideways at the walnut-faced market men squinting through smoke from their roll-ups, and the *nonnas* sitting in judgement like black toads.

'There are lots of good restaurants down by the sea, *signor*. Many of them have menus printed in French or English,' she added helpfully.

'I've heard that some places on the coast take advantage of the tourist dollar, and as I can actually speak a little Italian, *signorina*, the language won't necessarily be a problem for me.'

He smiled, and Sienna could believe it.

'In which case, the best place is twenty or thirty minutes' drive out of town. And it's quite a walk to the cab rank from here.'

Especially in shoes like those, she thought, her gaze firmly fixed on his Guccis.

'That won't necessarily matter. I was going to hire a car and invite some old friends out for lunch while I'm in their neighbourhood.'

The urge to look up at him grew too strong, so Sienna

gave in. A change had come over his expression. It was as though a cloud had passed in front of the sun, and she realised he disliked giving out information about himself.

Sienna nervously passed the tip of her tongue over her lips. 'The only thing is…the restaurant I recommended really needs somebody in your party who has an ear for the local dialect. Perhaps your friends are fluent, *signor*? Il Pettirosso is remote, and very much a haunt of those "in the know", as I think the saying goes. Are you sure you wouldn't be better off going to one of the fashionable places down by the sea after all? They get so much business from tourists that it's accepted all their staff will speak English. All sorts of famous people go there,' she finished lamely, in case he was famous, too, and she simply hadn't recognised him. With those expectant eyes and resolute mouth, he looked as though he should have an international fan club.

'I loathe watching money being thrown around solely in the hope of making an impression,' he announced. 'I prefer good food and service in excellent company. In which of your suggested places would *you* choose to eat?'

'If I could go anywhere?' Sienna could hardly imagine such luxury.

'Go anywhere, spend anything—I don't care what it costs as long as it's value for money.'

'Oh, then that's easy!' Sienna warmed with the thought of it. 'Il Pettirosso—even if it means buying a phrasebook to help with the ordering. It's a wonderful place with smoked glass windows so passers-by can't see inside. They specialise in local dishes, and everything is freshly prepared from the finest ingredients. Regional food is cooked there to the highest possible standard.'

His smile returned. 'That sounds just my sort of place. Authentic cuisine and an authentic name!'

'It's actually a sort of bird, *signor*. They live in the woodlands, and I shouldn't think you would ever see one inside Il Pettirosso. Unless they have pictures of them on the menu, of course.'

Putting his head on one side, he looked at her acutely. 'Are you telling me you've never actually eaten there?'

Sienna shook her head. The thought of trying to get her late husband Aldo over the threshold of a place like that made her smile.

The stranger reached inside his jacket and pulled out a small mobile phone. Flipping it open, he handed it to Sienna. She looked at him in bewilderment.

'Go on, then—the choice is made. Would you mind booking it for me, please, *signorina*? I might have a problem making myself understood if I can't give them some visual clues. I'll need a table for four at midday. That will give me plenty of time to make all the other arrangements.'

'I shall need a name, *signor*.'

'Oh, just tell them it is for Garett Lazlo,' he said, as though giving her the answer to everything.

Sienna's eyes widened at this, but she rang the restaurant as instructed. To her amazement, the booking was accepted straight away. Within seconds the formalities were complete. Next moment, the receptionist at Il Pettirosso was thanking her for the call with a warm goodbye. For a few precious seconds Sienna could fool herself that she was his glamorous personal assistant, making an official business call.

The phone was warmed by a faint fragrance of handsome Mr Lazlo. Sienna savoured it for as long as she could, until she had to hand it back.

'And now, *signorina*—can you achieve a double triumph, and point me in the direction of a decent car?'

Garett Lazlo tucked the phone back inside his jacket, all set to go. The part of Sienna that was not still under the influence of his masculine aroma almost managed to feel relieved.

'If you go straight through the market, then turn right and carry on across town, there is a prestige hire firm within a kilometre. Keep your back to the harbour and you can't miss it,' she said quickly.

'Thank you.'

It sounded as though there was a smile in his voice, but Sienna did not trust herself to check. When she eventually raised her head her visitor was strolling away, his jacket slung over one shoulder. With an unfamiliar pang of excitement she realised she could stare at him openly now, because everyone else in the market was doing exactly the same thing. Among that gallery, one more person admiring the tall, slim stranger would go unnoticed. Even if that person was 'poor, downtrodden Sienna', as everyone called her when they thought she could not hear.

She dared herself to take in his appearance for a few more minutes. There were always plenty of foreigners in Portofino, but this one was definitely something special. As she watched him walk away, Sienna was reliving every word he had spoken to her. Their conversation ran through her mind on an endless loop—his self-confidence, and her hesitancy. Butterflies were dancing in her stomach, although he had probably forgotten her almost instantly. He was looking over the other stalls again, and with genuine interest. The morning sunlight glowed against the dazzling white of his shirt. In contrast, his hair was gypsy-dark. Only a slight natural curl softened the depths of its carelessly expensive cut. Sienna found herself wondering what it would be like to trail her fingers through its luxuriance. The thought alarmed her, and she tried to look away. But it was hopeless. She had no choice but to watch him furtively until he was right out of sight, around the corner.

He never looked back. In contrast, Sienna spent the next hour glancing around for him.

It was still early in the day, and the season had barely started. Although there were a lot of visitors to Portofino, business was quiet. Sienna tried to keep her mind off the handsome American, but it was difficult. He had stirred a strange yearning in her. She made work for herself— arranging and rearranging the items on the co-op's table. Handmade lace produced in her village was always popular, and now that Molly Bradley was learning to make it as well, there would be no shortage of things to sell.

Kane and Molly Bradley were new arrivals in Piccia— polite, and not at all pushy. Sienna had first met them in the local store, where their 'teach yourself' Italian had earned them nothing but mutinous stares from the staff. Once Sienna had sorted everything out, the Bradleys had slowly but surely worked their way towards acceptance by the villagers.

The best sort of incomers were like that. They felt they had to work twice as hard as the locals to be thought half as good. Sienna did not mind newcomers, as long as they were like Kane and Molly. At least *they* weren't keeping holiday homes empty for most of the year, or playing at farming on the hills.

* * *

Sienna was wondering whether to pour herself a cup of coffee when someone spoke, making her jump guiltily.

'Hello again, *signorina*—I'd like to thank you for your directions. They were perfect.'

There was no mistaking that voice. It was like mountain honey. With dread in her heart, but hope in her eyes, Sienna straightened up to be confronted by all her dreams and nightmares rolled into one handsome package. That old woman back at home had been right when she'd said pirates had landed today, Sienna thought, as the fluttering feeling rose up from her stomach and turned all her sensible thoughts into butterflies.

She did not dare acknowledge the stranger with anything more than a nod. He took no notice of her nervous silence. Leaning forward, he planted his hands firmly on the edge of the table. He made it instantly obvious that, whatever he had come for, it was not souvenirs.

'Don't mention it,' Sienna said, turning hot pink as she felt the eyes of all the other stallholders fastening on her. She was already thinking of this stranger as 'The Pirate' so the thrust behind his next words should have come as no surprise—but it did.

'I've got the hire-car, and as none of the phrasebooks on sale in town included detailed directions to Il Pettirosso, I'm here to collect *you*.' He homed in on her with a devastating smile.

'Me?' Sienna stared around, flustered. Everyone was looking. She was the centre of attention, which she hated, but at least they were all smiling.

'It's the perfect solution, *signorina*. You'll be able to

make sure I get there on time, in one piece, and by the most direct route.'

Distracted, Sienna plucked at her skirt. If Garett Lazlo had been one of the regular guys who cruised the stalls on the lookout for lone girls that would have been easily fixed. She had no hesitation in telling strangers where to go. But this man was different. He was serious, formal, and truly stunning—and for the moment at least he seemed to have eyes only for her.

Sienna began to panic. She ached to break free from her boring life and do something different, but her reputation was on the line. She imagined all the elderly Ligurian matrons in their doorways and loggias, on their stalls and balconies, shaking their heads and sucking their remaining teeth in disapproval. She could almost feel their eyes boring into her. One wrong move, one word out of place, and Sienna was sure her honour would be gone for ever. She had not felt so totally alone since her wedding day.

Garett Lazlo smiled again. Sienna did not need to look up and see it. Her heightened senses were already filling in the details of his irresistible face and those tempting dark eyes...

If only she was free. She wished with all her heart that the world would go away and let her be herself for once. But who *am* I? she thought helplessly. It's been years since I've been allowed to give it any thought. So now I'm nothing but a girl who is too scared to say yes. Even to a once-in-a-lifetime offer like this!

'Don't tell me you're going to resist coming along for the ride?' he said silkily. 'I've picked up *such* a car. It's beautiful—sleek and shiny—and it is exactly the same shade of Mediterranean blue as your eyes.'

'How do you know, *signor*?'

Despite her nerves, this man aroused strange, conflicting feelings inside her, and she felt she had to challenge him.

'My attention to detail is said to be legendary. But allow me to check—'

Before Sienna knew what was happening, cool, strong fingers had slipped beneath her chin and tilted up her head. In the last hour she had agonised over Garett Lazlo's approach, and then been struck dumb by his presence. But such intimacy from this stranger cleared her mind in a flash. She jumped back, cannoning into her stall. As she did so her vacuum flask overbalanced, bounced off the corner of the table and landed with a shuddering thump in her open lunchbox. Coffee and sparkling shards of glass spilled out over the focaccia and salad she had been about to eat.

For one second everyone looked at the scene in shocked silence. Then Sienna drew in a great breath and rounded on the American. 'Oh, *look* what you've done!'

Garett spread his hands in an artless gesture. 'What can I say? I am sorry—but I didn't expect you to act like a frightened rabbit. All I did was make a perfectly reasonable request for you to accompany me to an appointment as my guide and interpreter. I may have backed it up with a little harmless flirtation, but if you aren't in the market for that—well, it's fine by me.' He shrugged one shoulder, unconcerned by what he deemed to be her overreaction.

Sienna had to concentrate hard to stop her eyes filling with tears. She was hungry, and she didn't have any cash on her.

'My food is ruined,' she said in a small voice.

The way she spoke provoked a slightly amused expression.

'Problem solved—you're lunching with me.'

'He's got you there. You can't argue with that!' One of the *nonnas* nodded with satisfaction.

Sienna had been scared of the elderly ladies who manned the other market stalls. Now she turned to stare at this one with open amazement. The old woman grinned back at her.

'He's ruined your lunch. A girl must eat—so the least he can do is feed you!'

'Thank you, *signora*,' Garett replied to the bystander, whose intonation worked in any language. He looked back at Sienna in obvious triumph. 'The fact is, *signorina*, you need a lunchtime break and some refreshment. I need directions and a translator. If I take you to lunch now, that will solve all our problems—yours and mine. Therefore I am your perfect lunch companion, and you are mine.'

'No, I'm not! I don't know… I can't…' Sienna struggled, wishing she could say yes but knowing she would never allow herself to do so.

Garett Lazlo met all her excuses with amusement, which gave her no help at all.

'Il Pettirosso has a strict dress code…it is that sort of place. I couldn't possibly walk in there dressed like this!' She flipped her fingers over the plain black of her clothes. This expanded his smile still further.

'I don't see why not. Black is always in fashion.' His gaze travelled slowly down from her face in cool appraisal. 'It's true that your clothes are a little austere, *signorina*, but as far as I am concerned less is more in that department. Especially when it can be dressed up so easily.' He threw his glance across the handicrafts on her table and it stopped when he saw a beautiful angora wrap. It was as blue as an angel's eyes and as insubstantial as gossamer. Picking it up, he swept it in a misty billow around her shoulders, arranging it gently against her neck.

For those few precious seconds Sienna was enveloped in his clean, masculine fragrance once again. Intoxicated now, as well as astonished, she watched him in silence. He was casting a connoisseur's eye over the delicate jewellery she had brought to sell. When he lifted a fine filigree of silver from her display, and held it up to catch the dancing sunlight, she knew there would be no resisting his next suggestion—whatever it was.

'Now, all you need is this lapis necklace and matching bracelet and there will be no one at Il Pettirosso—no matter how sophisticated the place might be—who can raise a candle to you, *signorina*,' he said calmly, handing it to her.

Thank goodness he didn't try to put it on me, Sienna thought, almost deafened by the sound of her heart hammering against her ribs. She hesitated at the sight of the beautiful necklace in her hands. It glittered and tempted her like cool water in a drought.

'Yes…but I really cannot let you do this, *signor*!' She shook her head and turned away, thinking of the craftsmen and women back in Piccia. They were depending on her to make them some money. 'All these things are for sale. They aren't here to act as a dressing up box for me. I can't possibly use them! And what would I tell the co-operative—that I just danced off for lunch when I should have been taking care of business here?'

She put one hand up to her neck, touching the place where the beautiful necklace would have lain against her skin. She ached, and hoped it was because she wanted to feel the kiss of its metal there, rather than Garett Lazlo's lips. That did not bear thinking about.

As her fingers fluttered over the smooth lines of her collarbone a shaft of sun streaked over the golden band on her wedding finger. Garett leaned back. It was only a slight movement, but it released Sienna from his shadow. Glancing up, she waited to feel relief that he no longer seemed about to force his presence on her. But when it came, the feeling was tinged with the faintest trace of disappointment.

'I have a duty to the people who sent me here, *signor*,' she said quietly.

'Your loyalty does you credit, *signora*. But you have overlooked one simple fact. I'm not asking you to do anything immoral. Accompany me to lunch now, and I shall pay for all the things you are borrowing from your stall. When we return you will give me an estimate of the money you might reasonably have expected to make in the length of time you have been away. What could be fairer than that?'

'Nothing!' one of the stallholders called out.

Sienna looked around at the *nonnas* and market men. The thought that they were waiting for her to step out of line had been terrifying her for weeks. It was true that they were all watching her today, but it was with interest and genuine amusement. None of them looked in the least bit disapproving.

'I'd go with him like a shot if I was fifty years younger!' a nearby stallholder suggested. She was a tiny, bird-like woman, grinning up from her knitting.

'Do you think it would be all right, *signora*?' Sienna asked doubtfully.

The old lady rested the lacy beginnings of a matinee jacket in her lap. Loosening another length of baby-pink wool from the skein in her enormous carpetbag, she looked up with a mischevious twinkle.

'My long life has taught me that you should grab opportunity with both hands whenever it shows up. And especially if it looks like him!' She gestured with one long, fine knitting needle. Everyone within earshot laughed out loud.

Garett Lazlo studied them all as though his face was carved in stone. 'Did I understand that correctly, *signora*?'

'N-no. Probably not.' She hoped.

'I certainly hope you did, *signor*!' The *nonna* chuckled with delight, speaking in heavily accented English this time. 'Take her away with a clear conscience, *signor*, and for as long as you like. I shall look after her stall.'

'Thank you.' Garett inclined his head graciously and took a firm hold on Sienna's elbow.

'She speaks English?' he queried, drawing Sienna quickly across the marketplace before she had time to think up any more delaying tactics.

'We all do. If the price is right.' But as she said the words she worried that he would take them the wrong way. Had she just wrecked her own reputation?

CHAPTER TWO

THEY were leaving the busy market behind. He was drawing her away from the crowds. If she were forced to call for help, then soon there would be no one to hear her. Panic began to bubble up, foaming into real fear. Garett Lazlo was so much bigger than she was. Fighting him off, if worse came to the worst, would not be an option.

Sienna did the only thing she could. Stopping abruptly, she caught him off balance.

'Wait—I wasn't expecting you to take me to lunch, Mr Lazlo, much less anything else. I'm not looking to make anything out of this at all—honestly! If you are going to regret dressing me up like this, then you should know that I made this wrap, and my friend designed and made the jewellery. I can pay her back for that, and at least no one but me will be any the poorer if my wrap has to be given away, rather than sold. It won't cost you a thing. I can easily make the co-operative another one.'

'You made this?'

She nodded, on firm ground for once. 'I keep rabbits for meat. It is easy to hide a few Angoras in their shed as well.' Sienna warmed with the thought of that tiny triumph, which she had managed in the face of Imelda and Aldo. Neither of them would have recognised a rabbit outside of a casserole dish.

Intrigued, he lifted the trailing edge of the cornflower-blue shrug and inspected the fine stitches. 'It's exquisite. And you look ravishing in it, by the way,' he added disarmingly. 'But I find dedication and skill like this in one so young slightly worrying. A beautiful woman like you really should get out more, *signora*.'

'I'm not allowed—that is, I don't get the chance. I have to keep house for my stepmother on top of everything else,' Sienna corrected herself quickly. Imelda might treat her like Cinderella, but she did not want this real-life Prince Charming to think she was a push-over—especially if they were about to enter a secluded alleyway together. 'That doesn't leave me the time or the energy for anything else,' she finished primly.

'I see.'

Her message must have been clear enough, for his grip on her elbow eased slightly. To Sienna's relief, he let go completely as they entered the warren of streets leading out of town.

She thought it was because he respected the line she had drawn between them, but Garett's mind was actually elsewhere. He was uneasy. His escape from Manhattan had been so sudden, and it meant travelling without the comfort of a schedule. His working days used to run like clockwork, but that was behind him for the moment. The alphabet soup of PAs, PDAs and GPS which made sure he got from A to B and back again in the shortest possible time was nothing but a memory. He patted his jacket, feeling the reassuring bulge made by his passport. With that, and his unlimited funds, Garett could do what he liked and go where he wanted. The world should be his oyster. But he was finding freedom unexpectedly hard work.

This thought carved furrows in his brow. He had more money to burn than most people made in a lifetime, and yet it was no longer enough. Why not? Something—some basic truth obvious to everyone else—still evaded him. From the age of six he had worked continuously—because when he stopped the restlessness returned. A vital element was missing from his life. He had discovered a disturbing new side to himself earlier that week. It had made him realise he *must* find out what he lacked—immediately— but how? Work was clearly part of the problem. The only way he could think to avoid its siren song was to put a few thousands miles and complete radio silence between him and his headquarters. The moment he tried to log in to the office computer system his staff would be on his case like kids mobbing a tomcat. He needed space, and time to think.

Garett put one hand in his pocket. It was only the third time he had checked for the hire-car keys since they'd been handed to him. He must be slowing down. As he thought that, he noticed another change in himself. Strolling through these airless city passageways with a nervous stranger should have been hell—a horrible reminder of what he had escaped. Instead, he found himself actually enjoying the sensation of not being expected to make conversation. What was happening to him?

Without realising it, he slowed his walk still further. It gave him the chance to look around for once. Lifting his gaze from the pavement, he sent it up to where the

tenement canyons showed a strip of sky. The silhouette of
a woman with bulky breasts and a wayward home perm
loomed out of an upstairs window. She was holding a big
juice container. With a shout of cheerful warning she
poured water from it into her flower boxes. A noisy cascade
of liquid ran out from beneath her billowing scarlet
geraniums, darkening the front of the apartment block
before dripping down to the flagstones.

A trickle ran towards the feet of Garett's unwilling
companion. She was lost in thought and had not noticed
the gardener overhead. Now she looked up and frowned at
the clear, cloudless sky above.

'An April shower?' Garett spoke his thoughts aloud.
Then he smiled, realising that for the first time in decades
he was thinking about something other than work.

It might not be the whole answer to his problems.

But it was a start.

The car was every bit as beautiful as he'd said it would be.
Sienna slid into the passenger seat with a sigh of real longing.

'Good, isn't it?' He smiled, slipping behind the wheel
with similar satisfaction.

Sienna nodded, but did not speak. She was determined
to keep her head down. Garett Lazlo had not laid a finger
on her since letting go of her arm. Whatever her secret
feelings about that, she knew she must not encourage him
in any way. But modesty was not the only reason for her
silence. On the way to the restaurant they would be passing
within a few kilometres of Piccia. She could only hope and
pray that none of the villagers saw her being driven along
in a car like this.

Although I'm the last person anyone would expect to see in a Lamborghini. She smiled to herself. They'd probably write it off as a hallucination, brought on by too much sun.

'You're the first girl who's ever smiled at my driving. They usually squeal and grab at something.' Garett glanced at her as he pulled away from the kerb. 'What's the joke?'

'N-nothing,' she said nervously, 'except that…travelling along like this reminds me of that old song: "If My Friends Could See Me Now". I was wondering what my stepmother would say if she caught sight of me in this!' She ran her hand lovingly over the passenger seat. It was made from softest glove-leather, and had the fragrance of money well spent.

His face cleared, and his eyes narrowed with devilment.

'Let's call in on her and find out, shall we?'

Sienna was horrified. 'No! Please don't! She would kill me! Respectable women aren't seen in fast cars with strange men.'

'Why not? Better that, surely, than being spotted in a strange car with a fast man? Are we going to pass your house?'

'No—thank goodness,' Sienna said with real feeling. 'It's too far from here to take a detour without making you late for your table reservation, *signor*.'

'I get the message—you're keeping me safely at arm's length. But that's no reason to be so formal. You can call me Garett.'

Sienna's lips flickered briefly into a smile. Then it was gone and she looked out of her window again. This was not what he had come to expect from women.

'Don't you have a given name, *signora*?' he prompted her.

'Of course, but perhaps we should keep this formal.' Sienna pursed her lips.

'I call all the ladies of my acquaintance by their first names, so why not give me yours?'

Sienna took this as an order. She was used to those, but it didn't make carrying them out any easier. Besides, this was a total stranger. She had to make a stand somehow, and insist on keeping him at a distance. Resisting would overturn everything she had been taught about obedience—but the idea excited her. She had already done one astonishing thing today, by coming this far with him. Why not another?

'My name is Signora di Imperia.' She looked at Garett boldly, daring him to challenge her for more information.

One hand on the steering wheel, he watched her with interested eyes. Sienna returned his look. And then, almost imperceptibly, he smiled. Then he transferred his gaze to the road ahead. As he did so, he gave the same small, formal bow of his head he had given the respectable matron back in the market place.

Sienna knew now why the old woman had giggled like a teenager. Garett Lazlo's talent for melting women with his smallest gesture was at work on her, too. Oh, if only they could exchange more than pleasantries…

After Garett pulled his car into Il Pettirosso's car park and killed the ignition, he drew out his mobile and made a quick call before getting out.

'First they're engaged. Now they've switched their damned answering machine on!' he announced.

Sienna flashed a look at him. His lips were a taut line. A pulse was beating visibly at his temple. But when he finally spoke into the phone his confident tone was in total contrast with his strained features.

'It's me,' he said, without bothering to explain who 'me' was. 'The time is eleven fifty-nine a.m., Tuesday. I'm sitting in Il Pettirosso with my credit card in my hand just waiting to entertain you. So if you want to make the most of this outrageous offer, you'll get down here for lunch ASAP!'

He ended the call, and then clicked his tongue in disappointment. Shoving the phone back into his pocket, he slammed the door of his hire-car with a report that echoed across the nearby valley like a gunshot. Sienna gulped. As they walked the few metres from his car to the smoked glass door of the restaurant she hoped he would not need her to do much translating for him. If he was cross already, he might not take kindly to having the menu deciphered for him as though he was illiterate.

She need not have worried. They followed in the restaurant manager's highly polished footsteps to a discreetly placed table for four. Sienna was gazing around in awe at the clean, modern lines of the restaurant, but Garett had his eyes on something much more down to earth.

'Ah—so that's what a *pettirosso* is!' He pointed to the beautifully painted European robin on the front of his menu. 'Do you know, there's a duke in England who has one of these living in the grounds of his historic house that will actually hop onto his hand to be fed?'

Sienna watched him for a minute to see if he was joking. But his smile seemed quite genuine, and she decided to probe further.

'How do you know?'

'He does it as a kind of party trick to impress visitors.

I think the poor old guy's lonely. He valued me as much as someone to talk to as a business advisor.'

Sienna raised her eyebrows and lowered her head to study the menu. She did not want Garett to see her amazement at what he had said. A man who talked to dukes was sitting opposite her in the restaurant of her dreams! She tried to concentrate on the list of dishes before her, but that made her feel still more nervous. Il Pettirosso offered everything from asparagus to zucchini. She had no idea what to select, nor—more importantly—how much of his money Garett would be willing to spend on her.

'Choose what you like, Signora di Imperia.' he announced, as though reading her thoughts. 'If a place is good value for money, I don't bother with budgeting. Just order, and I'll see to the rest. For myself, I've been living off chateaubriand and fries for days, so I think I'll make it something vegetarian for my main course. I fancy a change today.' He lifted one shoulder in an easy gesture.

Vegetarian—that sounded reassuringly cheap. Sienna decided to order the same thing he did, but went on pretending to study the menu. This was partly to give his friends time to arrive, but also because it was a rare luxury. Sienna had not been out to lunch for years, and certainly never to a bewitching place like this. The experience ought to be played out for as long as she could manage.

Poring over the deckle-edged, beautifully inscribed menu, she waited until, despite his obvious good manners, Garett showed signs of becoming a little restless. Eventually she looked up shyly. He smiled and summoned the waiter.

'What have you chosen, Signora di Imperia?'

Sienna stopped smiling. 'Oh…er…actually, it all

looks so good I was hoping you could give me some suggestions…Garett…'

'I think we need a few more moments to decide, *signor*.' Garett nodded to their waiter. The moment the man stalked away, Sienna's host leaned forward with the look of someone who was about to reveal a great secret.

'You were right, *signora*, this place might have been beyond me if I had come here on my own. I thought to follow *your* selection! I can recognise all the general words, for things like soup and pasta, but some of these regional names are beyond me. Could we perhaps puzzle them out between us?'

Laughing, they went through the choices together, and came up with *cacciucco* for their starter, with *pansôti al preboggion* to follow. Sienna stayed with her idea of choosing the same things he did. It made ordering easier, and gave her a few extra seconds to gaze around in awe at her surroundings—and, more secretively, at her host.

The headwaiter materialised beside Garett the moment they were ready. Sienna looked up and smiled a little apprehensively as the man flourished his silver fountain pen over a small leatherbound notepad.

'Don't worry. I'll do the ordering,' Garett said smoothly, before she could open her mouth.

She held her breath, waiting to see what would happen.

His pronunciation was faultless. Before Sienna could congratulate him, a telephone call from his mobile burst in between them.

'Darn—it seems like we're going to be lunching on our own after all, *signora*. My friends can't make it,' he said when he had taken the call. He clicked his tongue, and then smiled at her reaction. 'What's the matter? Anyone would think you weren't looking forward to eating here in your dream restaurant.'

'It isn't that.' Sienna watched him switch off his phone and tuck it away. Suddenly it was as though the shrinking market girl had returned, trying to take up as little room as possible at his table. 'I had not expected to be dining alone with you.'

He narrowed his eyes in a way that made her smile, despite her nerves. 'That cuts both ways, you know, *signora*. But I suppose we're both going to have to buckle down and endure it.' He sighed theatrically, making Sienna giggle.

As her laughter died away, the sophisticated silence of the restaurant closed in. Garett was completely at ease. He sat back and studied his surroundings openly. Sienna could not manage to look anywhere directly, taking small swift glances around the room when she thought no one else was looking. Her mind was as active as her eyes, although it was not doing her much good. She desperately wanted to start up a witty, sparkling conversation. Only two things stopped her. Not being able to look at him without blushing was bad enough, but the second reason was still more of an obstacle.

She could not think of a single sensible thing to say. But then she was rescued by the most unlikely of sources. A butterfly flitted in through an open window of the restaurant.

'Oh, look—an orange tip!'

'You know about butterflies, *signora*?' He quirked a brow, suitably impressed.

'Not really, but they've increased at home since the place

has been allowed to run wild. They like the purple flowers that have seeded themselves all the way through the old terrace walls. The name is one I like, too—easy and obvious.'

Sienna almost felt she might be about to relax, but the arrival of their wine and first course put a stop to that. Her stomach contracted to the size of a split pea again. As usual, Garett took the attentions of the staff in his stride. Even before they swept away he leaned over his dish and inhaled appreciatively.

'Ah—so *cacciucco* must be fish soup, Signora di Imperia?'

'That's right. I don't know how much you picked up from the menu, but it said all the restaurant's raw materials are brought in fresh each morning. They come from a few kilometres away at the coast, or from local farms and smallholdings.'

He paused while breaking his bread, and leaned towards her with an enigmatic look on his face.

'I saw that. It made me realise that the ordinary people around here have to make things, as you do, or wrestle produce out of their surroundings. The menu really brought it home to me.' He paused again, considering what a strange word 'home' was in his circumstances. He tried to laugh again, but it came out as a harsh, dry sound. 'I ate nothing but junk until I managed to make a better life for myself. The chance to eat fresh local food in a place like this is a luxury.'

Sipping at a spoonful of her soup, Sienna regarded him. His mouth was a grim line now, and his eyes were hard as he stared past her into space.

'Perhaps it is all this home-grown fresh food in Liguria that keeps us so good-tempered?' she risked, testing his mood.

That broke Garett's trance. A puzzled frown flickered across his features, and he looked down at his clenched hand as though it belonged to someone else. Sienna noticed that it took him a conscious effort to relax his fingers. She went on watching him from beneath her lashes, and as she did so he began to lose the hunched tension that made him look like a prizefighter. He picked up his spoon, but to Sienna's relief did not actually attack his meal. He skimmed the *cacciucco* with graceful, economical movements.

Relieved, she concentrated on her own lunch. Even so, he had completely finished before she dared to speak again.

'I wish I had more of the killer instinct,' she said, almost making it sound casual. 'It would make an event like this less of an ordeal for me.' She tried to laugh, but it did not work.

'Fine dining is supposed to be a pleasurable experience.' Tipping his bowl away from him, he finished the last of his soup. Then he laid down the spoon. His every movement seemed measured to Sienna, as though he was unable to relax for a moment.

'Do you enjoy it, *signor*?'

'In the right company, yes.'

'Then it is a shame your friends are not here.'

'Oh, I'm doing fine, *signora*.'

He smiled, and the richness of his tone made Sienna wonder if he was only talking about lunch…

CHAPTER THREE

For once in his life, seduction was not on Garett's agenda. He was visiting Europe for a rest, not more of the same. He glanced across at her, the smile still teasing his lips. Seduction might be too much hassle at the moment, but fantasies…they were another thing altogether. He would find time for those instead.

As though reading his mind, the girl blushed and lowered her head. Amused, Garett went back to his meal. He did not anticipate any trouble from a casual lunch guest like this. She was intended as nothing more than visual entertainment for him. He liked to furnish his world with beautiful things, but, while he looked on works of art as investments to be studied as well as displayed, his women were different. They were like butterflies. They flitted into his life through one window of opportunity and out through the next. This one would be no different. If anything, she would make less impact on him than his usual pick-ups. Signora di Imperia was safe from everything but his active imagination—although he intended to let that run as free as it liked.

Garett went on watching her covertly. He was savouring the idea of stripping away her inhibitions one by one, as her shock and confusion melted into desire. It awakened in him a feeling that he thought would be hard to better—and then something happened that improved on it. She looked up as their main course arrived, and in a reflex action her tongue darted out to moisten her lips. Her anticipation fired Garett's—but for something far more pleasurable than mere food. He imagined her using that neat little pink tip to caress him all the way to paradise. As the waiter moved to his side of the table, Garett had to pull his chair in closer to the table to hide the most obvious sign of his arousal. Trying to distract himself, he stared down into the white porcelain dish of ravioli that had been placed before him. It was still bubbling, as hot as his thoughts.

A squeak from the other side of the table made him jerk his head up again. An eruption of sauce had splashed out and burned Signora di Imperia's hand. As he watched, she sucked her finger to cool the heat. But it did nothing to quell Garett's desire.

Then her gaze flew to his. Her blue eyes opened wide. Instantly she withdrew her finger and hid it in her lap.

'Oh—I am so sorry, *signor*! What can I say? It's just that…I'm so nervous. Coming to a place like this is such a novelty for me—I've never been anywhere so wonderful—'

'Don't mention it,' he murmured, his mind on something else entirely.

'Be careful—the dish is very hot. I hope you like it.'

'I'm sure I shall.' He smiled with complete conviction.

While waiting for his food to cool a little, Garett took a sip of wine and congratulated himself on his choice.

This Moscato was a light, yet aromatic example of its type. It perfectly complemented both their soup and now their main course. He counted himself lucky to be able to experience it. No, I've earned the right to do this, he corrected himself quickly. Garett was a strong believer in making his own luck. *Anybody* could do what he had done if they wanted success badly enough. When would people learn that all it took was hard work?

Then Garett realised his companion was dissecting her dish of pasta pillows in their velvety sauce in a particular way. It was a delaying tactic he recognised from his life on the streets. She had already told him that dining like this was out of her league. Now he sensed she was trying to make the experience last for as long as possible.

He could only hope there was not another, darker reason for her time-wasting. Watching her slender wrists and delicate hands as she toyed with her food, he wondered when she would next see a decent meal. An unlikely interest in some people's habits was another legacy of his deprived childhood.

Garett's frown of concern was enough to bring their waiter scurrying to his side.

'I wonder, could you bring me some more of this, please? And another serving of garlic bread?'

Sienna was so amazed, words burst from her before she could stop them.

'But you haven't touched what is in front of you yet, *signor*!'

'Good grief—that isn't the sort of reaction I'm used to from my dinner guests.' He laughed.

Sienna paused, and then shot a glance across at him.

He had turned on a particularly winning smile, aimed at the restaurant staff scurrying up with his additional order.

'It's all for you, *signora*,' he whispered. 'Enjoy!'

Plates were juggled and the table rearranged to make space for the extra dishes. Sienna was speechless, but at least the shock gave her time to consider her reply.

'This is very kind of you, Signor Lazlo,' she murmured as soon as all the waiters were out of earshot, 'but I'm sure I shall never manage all this. What made you think my own meal wasn't big enough?'

He shrugged. 'You're as thin as a rail, and white as paper. Eat up. The servings here may not be American-sized, but they'll still put some roses in your cheeks.'

'So…does that mean your own meal is too small?'

He began making great inroads into his own ravioli, with evident satisfaction.

'Not at all. I can never stand to see good food go to waste, so I always eat everything that is put in front of me.'

'It seems to do you good.'

The words were out before Sienna could stop them. She gasped, desperate to take them back, but Garett had heard too many empty compliments in his life to take much notice of hers. And he chuckled at her innocent remark.

'What I meant was…I mean, you look perfectly—that is…'

He let her flounder about, watching with amusement as she got more and more flustered, and more and more embarrassed. It pleased him to see a woman struggling over compliments. The girls who slinked up to him at parties all read from the same script. They had their patter worked out. This Signora di Imperia was anything but practised.

She was obviously attracted to him, but trying not to show it. This made a refreshing change for Garett. Though of course he would never respond to any come-on from a mousy little innocent like her! It was all he could do not to laugh out loud at the idea of it. What sort of attraction could she possibly hold for him?

The lure of the forbidden: the most powerful one in the world, his body told him suddenly, with an alarming jolt.

Disturbed, he looked up from his meal. Their eyes met across the table and he found himself looking temptation straight in the face. Suddenly the innocence in her large, clear eyes began to inflame rather than quell his feelings. The urge to stir those Mediterranean depths with desire—desire for him and him alone—was almost overwhelming…

But he wouldn't let that distract him now. He smiled lazily in her direction. 'Forget it, *signora*—I already have. Now, let's enjoy our delicious lunch!'

His unruly libido was not so easily distracted.

Their pudding was a wonderful shared confection of cream, chocolate mousse and chestnut puree.

'It's such a shame your friends weren't able to enjoy this lovely meal.' Sienna slumped in her seat with a sigh of satisfaction as coffee was served. Garett had been so charming over lunch that she was almost tempted to forget her suspicions about his motives. Then she thought of what Aldo would have said at such terrible backsliding, and sat up again smartly.

'I shouldn't waste too much sympathy on them, *signora*. We all eat like this far too often for our own good. It's the executive's plague.'

Sienna believed him, but could tell instinctively that this wasn't a man who overindulged too often. He liked to be in control. She suddenly had a delicious vision of him working his body in his private gym…

'I wish I could eat like this all the time.' She sighed with longing, dabbing her lips with her starched white napkin. Even that was luxury. The damask was so thick and perfect. She folded it neatly and dropped it beside her plate as her host summoned the waiter.

'But you can if you want to, *signora*,' Garett said softly as he paid the bill.

She looked up at him. Was this the moment he closed in on her? What would she say? What could she do? Resistance would be useless—but how could she possibly square it with her conscience, or keep it a secret, or—?

'All you have to do is get yourself a dream, then go all-out to seize it with both hands,' he went on smoothly.

Sienna might have been relieved—if she hadn't been so disappointed.

'That's easy for you to say, *signor*. Dreaming isn't going to pay my bills or put food on our table, is it?' She spoke quickly, trying to cover her confusion.

'It's worked OK for me.'

'Yes, but I live in the real world, *signor*.'

'So do I.'

He stood up to take possession of Sienna's wrap and draped it around her shoulders. As he did so, he half-turned to thank their waiter for his service. The movement threw her against Garett—their bodies touching and her lips only inches from his.

What happened next was almost too much for Sienna

to bear. With a gentle smile he lifted his hand and caressed it softly against her hair. This was the moment. The moment she had wished for, daydreamed about in the marketplace. For a heartbeat Sienna was paralysed with fear. She had been terrified that this might happen. She didn't know what to do or how to react. Instinctively she leapt away from him and ran like a frightened rabbit.

Garett watched her go, stunned. What was all *that* about?

'Well, that's a first!' he joked to their equally astonished waiter. 'I've never been abandoned by a girl before.'

'Don't take it personally, *signor*,' the man confided. 'Women don't like insects. It was just a reaction to feeling that butterfly on her head, that is all. She will return.'

But she didn't.

A few hours later, Garett was revelling in the amusement the tale of his lunchtime adventure was giving his hosts.

'I tell you, Kane, it was such a pity you couldn't make lunch today. You should have been there. All through the meal that girl looked at me as though I was trying to buy her soul. I had no intention whatsoever of coming on to her, but watching her wondering how on earth she was going to say no to me was priceless. And then I just moved to brush that butterfly away from her, and she vanished.'

'And when did any woman last say no to you, Garett?' Kane Bradley nudged his guest confidentially.

'I don't remember.'

'That's because it's never happened.' Kane's wife Molly chuckled indulgently, then stood up. 'But if you two are going to start talking dirty, I'm off to check on dinner.' She moved smoothly to the dining room door.

The moment she was out in the hall, she called for her butler.

'Is Sienna here yet, Luigi?'

'*Sì, signora*—I showed her straight upstairs to your dressing room.'

'Good. Did she manage to smuggle a decent dress from home to change into, do you know? Or will she be borrowing one of mine?'

Molly did not need an answer. The sight of her second dinner guest appearing on the first-floor landing silenced all her questions.

Sienna looked stunning in a perfectly plain black evening dress. Its plunging neckline and sleek, stark lines were accentuated by a glitter of diamonds at her neck and a worried look in her eyes.

'You look absolutely wonderful!' Molly rushed forward to brush a kiss against Sienna's cheek as she reached the bottom of the stairs. Slipping an arm around her friend's narrow waist, the hostess led her across the hall. 'Now, don't forget—your job is to bring a little local colour into the life of one of Kane's oldest friends. We're worried about him. There's something wrong, but he's not a guy who makes a lot of fuss. He won't tell, and we know better than to pry. At least we've managed to persuade him to stay here with us for a while. His original idea was to work his way around the Med, but it's clear he needs more than that. You'll see it as soon as you look at him. And, as we don't speak Italian fluently yet, I thought you would be the perfect bridge between him and the locals while he's here.'

Sienna allowed herself to be drawn along to the dining room. She was fretting about everything—from the excuses she had made at home to the unfamiliar make-up she had applied so hurriedly in the borrowed dressing room. 'You know I'd do anything to help you, Molly, but if my stepmother finds out about this—'

'For goodness' sake, girl! You're twenty-six years of age. The mistress of your own house and estate. You don't need anybody's say-so!'

'Yes…but I'm still not sure…'

'Then the least you can do is come in and enjoy a good dinner with us while you make up your mind.' Molly gave her reluctant guest a gentle shake, and put her hand to the dining room door.

Garett was trying to let the future take care of itself for once, but one thing still bothered him. For some reason he had been unable to shake off the memory of Signora di Imperia. Until now, no woman had ever lingered long in his memory. They passed through and vanished with all the speed of happy thoughts. But images of the girl from Portofino would not let him go. Speaking about her to Kane and Molly had been his way of exorcising her image, but it had not worked. It was beginning to irritate him. He could not forget the woman, and it was no longer funny.

He tapped the rim of his cocktail glass, unable to concentrate on the conversation in hand. As his host talked, Garett's mind wandered far away. What was she doing right now? He had waited for her, and he had worried—two notable firsts for Garett. Learning that she had got a lift back to Portofino market with one of the restaurant's cleaners had not really satisfied him. He needed to know that she had returned safely. Thoughts of what might have happened to her had been distracting him all day. It was proving impossible to pull his thoughts away from that girl. Especially when the alternative was listening to Kane's tale about some old dame living in the villa next door.

Garett took another drink, and tried to concentrate on what his friend was telling him. As a favoured guest, it was the least he could do. Relaxation was impossible for him, but the Bradleys were old friends, and they were trying so hard. He owed it to them to make an effort—right down to discreetly investigating the financial situation of the respectable widow who would be joining them for dinner that evening. He accepted another vermouth from Kane, and nodded as his host droned on about their worries for this Sienna.

The open fire crackling in the hearth had warmed Garett from the moment he'd first walked in. Whether it could thaw the ice at his core was another matter. He went on letting his mind wander. It was supposed to head away from trouble, but it kept on veering towards the unattainable girl he had picked up in the market. Her quiet beauty had attracted him from right across the square, like a panther drawn to a fawn. But his recent escape from routine had stopped him following his usual well-worn path from banter to bedroom. He sighed. Sleeping with her would definitely have prevented her gaining such a hold over his mind. Giving in to instinct there and then would have stopped her image working its way under his skin so successfully.

On the surface, Garett seemed to be the perfect guest. He made small talk and nodded in all the right places as his host chatted. Yet behind this polite façade his mind was working. There was only one way to rid himself of his beautiful distraction. He would find that girl again. Whatever it took. He began to work out a plan of campaign. A suite in the Hotel Splendido would do it. If Il Pettirosso had impressed her, then a visit to that peach of a place would guarantee her fall. And Garett would be there to catch her in his arms.

All he had to do now was track her down again.

That might take time. He already knew that separate markets were held on different days. For any other man, there would be no guarantee she could be found. But success for Garett was a mere formality. He was already drawing up details of where to go and who to see in the search for his shy interpreter when something momentous happened. It was something that had him mentally screwing up all his plans and kicking them into touch.

He wouldn't have to bother going all the way to Portofino—visiting markets and asking around— because his mystery girl was walking straight into the room to meet him.

CHAPTER FOUR

GARETT considered himself to be the complete master of his emotions. People only saw what he wanted them to see. So when the shimmering vision of Sienna di Imperia was formally introduced to him, Garett's calming, confident smile was already in place.

'It's my beautiful lunch guest—with a beautiful name to match. Well, I can certainly vouch for her honour, Kane, if not for mine.'

'Then you've met before?' Molly Bradley's eyes were twinkling. 'You never told us, Sienna.'

'I didn't realise your guest was going to be Mr Lazlo.' Sienna tried to remain cool, but her temperature was already rising.

'This makes it two prestige meals in one day for us, Molly. It's a pleasure to see you again Signora di Imperia.' Garett stepped forward and took Sienna's hand. Raising it to his lips he brushed it with the lightest of formal kisses— but his eyes were alight with devilment.

'This is the first time we have been formally introduced,' Sienna said with as much dignity as she could manage in the face of the surrounding smiles.

All she wanted to do was run and hide, but she had promised to make Molly's guest feel welcome. She had to follow through, however alarmed she felt.

'I told Mr Lazlo he might need an interpreter for his lunch at Il Pettirosso. When he asked me to act for him, he was not expecting to eat alone,' she added meaningfully.

'But I'll bet he soon made up for our absence. That's our Garett!' Kane rocked back on his heels, laughing. 'He never lets a pretty girl slip through his fingers. Molly must have encouraged you to get all dressed up this evening. She's incorrigible.'

'No.' Sienna's blush deepened.

Spending her lunch hour being tempted by the presence of Garett Lazlo had been bad enough. Now, good manners had cornered her in a far worse situation. She had already lied to her stepmother that evening, and said she was going out for a walk. That was hardly innocent, but now she was being drawn deeper and deeper into a web of deception—and it was all Molly's fault.

'Actually, Molly is such a perfect hostess that she was probably worried that three for dinner was an awkward number. I live just down the lane, so it was convenient to invite me. I'm afraid I must have been the only person available, Mr Lazlo.'

'Don't do yourself down, Signora di Imperia.' He smiled. 'I prefer to look on it as Molly's unfailing good taste. She's picked out the one girl I would have chosen myself. This is obviously my lucky night.' Garett made an expansive gesture towards her with his glass.

Sienna's colour deepened to Tuscany velvet. Inside, she was crumpled up with embarrassment, but he was clearly revelling in the situation. All his easy amusement triggered a reaction in her, making her want to stand her ground for once.

'I don't think so, Mr Lazlo,' she said with shy formality. 'My husband has only been dead for three months.'

Sienna's remark left a heavy silence in the air.

Garett drew his glass in towards him again, but took his time before taking a sip. Then he concealed his other hand in his pocket before replying.

'I offer you my condolences, Signora di Imperia,' he said at last.

Sienna nodded in acknowledgement. She had learned long ago that silence was the best defence when it came to her marriage. Even those who were most curious about her relationship with Aldo never pried beyond the distant, sad smile she spent ages perfecting in front of her dressing room mirror.

'Hey—I've just had a thought. Garett here works to help the aristocracy maximise their profits all the time, Sienna. He'd be just the man to cast an eye over your estate.'

'Kane!' His wife was horrified at such a tactless approach.

'Oh, I'm sure Mr Lazlo has far too many other calls on his time,' Sienna said as the Bradleys' butler called them in to dinner.

'Actually, I'm on a self-imposed sabbatical from my city office at the moment. So in theory I could be all yours, *signora*.'

Before Sienna could put a decent distance between them, Garett took her arm and escorted her into the dining room, along with their hosts.

'Then if you are on holiday, Mr Lazlo, I'm quite sure

the last thing you want to do is work.' Sienna smiled. It was an expression she had less practice in using, but the smile dazzled nonetheless.

'Don't be too sure.' He laughed, and then paused, 'I'm just a workaholic, I guess.' He laughed and patted her hand, but it wasn't only the gesture that set Sienna's nerves on edge. There had been a slight hesitation in Garett Lazlo's voice. He had thought twice about his words, and chosen them more carefully the second time. His reaction had been quicksilver, but not fast enough to fool Sienna. In that instant she realised Molly was right. However good a friend this Garett Lazlo was to them, he was hiding something.

Sienna felt curiosity glittering within her.

She would find out his secret. It was the least she could do for her friends Molly and Kane, she thought, with only a *tiny* shred of guilt.

They were to eat in the Bradleys' summer dining room. Lit by candles, the room basked in the warmth of the flickering light. The butler pulled out a chair as Sienna reached the table. While she was busy smoothing down her gown and unfolding her napkin, Garett took the seat next to hers.

She automatically shrank back as he moved in.

'I'm only straightening my jacket, *signora*,' he murmured. 'You should know by now that I am *almost* civilised.'

There was a twinkle in his watchful dark eyes that fanned the sparks of Sienna's interest. Warmth began to trickle through her veins. It suffused her cheeks and increased the power of the applewood fire glowing in the grate.

'Are you all right, *signora*? You seem rather flushed.' Garett raised an eyebrow quizzically. His eyes did not soften the gesture, and she realised that running away from him after lunch had raised an invisible barrier between them. Trying to convince herself that this was a good thing, she flicked the briefest of smiles in his general direction.

'I am fine, thank you, Mr Lazlo. It is just that I am not used to such lovely warmth when dining at home, that is all.'

'Then your house is cold, *signora*?'

Sienna looked away quickly. 'With only the two of us living there now, myself and my stepmother, there isn't any point in lighting a fire when summer is only a few weeks away.'

'It can still get chilly in the evenings. Would you like to borrow my jacket, *signora*?'

'Garett! You'll embarrass the poor girl!' Molly chortled with laughter as their smoked salmon starter arrived. 'Don't worry, Sienna—your recipe for *tagliata* is coming up next. Good red meat will satisfy the animal in him.'

Garett gave Sienna a look that warned her not to be too sure about that. She wondered what his real reaction would be to their main course. At lunch, he had implied he was sick of steak. Dining out in such luxury must be nothing but a tiresome chore for a man like this, she thought wryly and that made her remember how different her life was from his.

'We've got Sienna to thank for more than her way with beef this evening.' Molly smiled at Garett as the staff fussed around them. 'When we first moved here, the shopkeepers made out they couldn't understand us. Apparently, when our boys visited this place during the Second World War, some of them forgot to settle their debts. Memories are long in these parts, Garett. In the interests of international relations, Sienna suggested that Kane and I should suddenly remember a whole heap of relatives. By happy coincidence a lot of them were GIs who'd come over here in forty-four. And guess what? All their names matched up with the ones on those unpaid bills posted behind the counter. One fistful of euros later and, thanks to Sienna, all the shopkeepers for miles around now greet us like best buddies.'

'Hmm. You don't want them thinking you're a soft touch, Molly,' Garett warned, although he was looking at Sienna with intrigue in his eyes.

'They would certainly never make that mistake about you, Mr Lazlo.'

'I shall take that as a compliment, Signora di Imperia.'

Sienna wanted to say that was not how she had intended it, but something happened. Between thinking the words and saying them, she looked too directly into his eyes. That did it. Her heart flipped. It knocked all the air from her lungs and every sensible thought from her head. He was irresistible—and he was looking straight at her. A dangerous echo rang in her ears. Imelda had told her to catch herself a rich pirate. By accepting Molly's simple invitation to dine, Sienna was laying herself wide open to being used like that all over again.

But if Garett Lazlo really tried directing all his charm onto her, how could she possibly resist him?

Garett was never off duty. He knew exactly what was expected of him. Nothing would make the Bradleys happier than to see Garett focus his full power on Signora Sienna di Imperia that evening. Minutes earlier, the

Bradleys' guest of honour would have been only too happy to oblige. Now he was equally determined to resist. The last thing he needed now was a widow. He was trying to leave stress behind. This was not the time to shoulder someone else's emotional baggage, as well as his own heap of troubles.

At least the Widow di Imperia's scruples seemed almost equal to his own. His mind slipped back to the time they had spent over lunch. Her nervous restraint had been spiced with a flash of spirit when she ran away from him. Her frosty resistance tonight showed that core of steel again. She was sitting beside him as though her spine was a subway rail. Now she was within his reach, Garett could have purged her from his mind in an instant if he had chosen. A few moments of flirtation and she would be his. Once he got her into bed that would be it. All the magic she held for him would evaporate. It had happened to him so often in the past. Her hold over his subconscious would be broken. He would be free.

There was only one problem. He was not going to allow himself to do it. Sienna di Imperia was struggling to keep back the tide of financial disaster after the death of her husband. He knew that much from the Bradleys. He certainly didn't need any further hassle in his life. His solution would be to act his usual delightful self over dinner—while resolutely refusing to take any romantic bait laid for him either by his hosts or the lovely Sienna.

Resisting the impulse to seduce her was going to be torture. Garett smiled to himself. He loved a challenge. For him to pass up any pretty woman might be thought impossible. He knew better. As a businessman, he was invincible.

It was surely only a matter of applying cold, calculated best practice to the problem of Sienna di Imperia. He would concentrate his charm on Molly and Kane instead. The beautiful butterfly pinioned beside him would be treated to nothing more than the fallout from his brilliance.

A glass of champagne with the salmon underscored Garett's recent discovery that being entertained without strings felt good. The Bradleys never normally did this kind of thing because they wanted something from him. Tonight was an exception. They usually entertained him just because they liked him. As he considered this fact, the ghost of a frown crossed his face. Perhaps he *should* make room for a life outside of work. The problem was that Garett found it difficult to think of the way he earned a living as 'work'. It involved hours of conference calls, meetings, deadlines, travelling, jet lag and smiling until his jaws ached. The only time he realised how hard an act it was to maintain was when he stopped. That was why he *never* stopped. Real life only gave him the opportunity to think about things that were best left buried.

Garett Lazlo was famous as the man who outlawed holidays. He and his staff worked in shifts around the clock and around the year—with the exception of Christmas Day. He used that to catch up on his sleep and rediscover the trouble-free delight of carry-outs: dim sum, or brisket with latkes.

The event that had so recently driven him out of Manhattan was supposed to have changed his outlook. But it hadn't happened. He moved restlessly in his chair. It was too late for change, he told himself. Relaxation didn't fit easily with his image. Without constant mental and physical stimulation he felt uneasy. He knew for a fact that if you didn't keep on pushing, you slipped back. Growing up on the streets had taught him that. From his earliest days, Garett had heard all the people around him wishing their lives were different. It had made him realise he was unusual. Everyone else had that one single thing in common—they *wished*, but they didn't *do* anything to make their dreams come true. Garett had never been content with that. From the moment he'd learned how to sneak in and out unnoticed from his bunk at the children's home, he had set about carving out a better life for himself. The irony was, now that he had that better life, there wasn't any time left to enjoy it.

Garett had never wanted to give himself that time—until tonight. Now something had happened. All the screwed-up elements of his life must have tangled themselves to a standstill at last. The tensions of his past and present were meshed together in a standing wave, enabling him to find something strangely soothing about dining by candlelight. The meal was tolerable, and the company was unbeatable. Of course, it helped that he was sitting next to the most beautiful girl in the world—even if she was pretending to ignore him. That only made her all the more intriguing.

He might not allow anything to happen between them, but he could certainly admire and take his time over it. There was plenty to appreciate: the fragility of her, and the delicacy of her movements. Old Aldo di Imperia had been a lucky man. His young widow was beautiful, graceful, and intelligent company. They were precious qualities in themselves, but to find them combined in one woman was truly remarkable. Fortunately, Garett assured

himself, his dining companion was as loyal as she was
stunning. Her mouth, which was made for kissing, could
have been carved from coral. She might smile, but it
was never at him. Her glamorous black evening dress
accentuated the beautiful sweep of her spine, but she sat
in her seat as rigidly as an ice statue. The glory of her
auburn hair was piled high on her head, and at one point a
wayward curl escaped to coil against the creamy skin of
her neck. With any other woman, at any other time, Garett
would have made a great show of twining it back into its
pins for her. After what had happened at Il Pettirosso, it was
impossible to imagine doing such a thing to Signora Sienna
di Imperia. Even if he had been tempted…

'Molly tells me you live right next door to this place,
signora?' Garett picked up a crystal decanter of red wine
and filled a glass for her while the beef was being served.
'That must be convenient for visiting.'

'My house is actually about eight hundred metres away,
but we share a boundary fence, yes.'

She looked at him directly then, and he caught his lower
lip between his teeth to stop himself smiling at the sight.
It did not do full justice to her eyes to simply call them blue.
They were a colour in which a man could lose himself. A
susceptible man, he reminded himself. Dancing firelight
added a halo of gold dust around her large pupils. He gazed
into them, expecting the delicious shyness she had shown
at the market to lower those dark lashes again. He had a
long wait. Gradually it occurred to him that she wasn't
merely looking at him tonight. She was challenging him
now, in a way that other women never did. And that was
the reason Garett decided then and there to help her. She

had spirit, and that impressed him. And it was no hardship that that spirit came wrapped in a beautiful package!

Sienna smiled as she watched their hosts. The Bradleys were an ideal couple. As she looked at them, Kane speared a particularly succulent piece of steak on his fork and laughed, offering it to Molly. She accepted his donation, parting her scarlet lips with a full-throated giggle. Sienna looked away—and her gaze instantly locked with Garett's.

A tremor thrilled through her body—had he watched that touching little scene being acted out before them? How would it feel to have him indulge her like that, presenting her with food like a gift of love? Suddenly, her skin tingled with anticipation. A fine ecstasy of perspiration broke out all over her body. Flustered, she reached for her wine to break the moment—exactly as the butler moved forward to offer her a refill. In the confusion, her glass tumbled to the table. The last few drops of Barolo twinkled onto the tablecloth, glowing like blood against the luminous white. Despite their hosts' cries that it didn't matter, and the butler's practised efficiency, Sienna leapt into action, moving aside plates, cutlery, glasses and napkins to limit the damage.

'Don't let them embarrass you with all their happy-ever-after play-acting. The ties of love aren't as tight between them as you might think,' Garett murmured to her, under the guise of helping to mop up the wine.

Sienna stopped and stared at him. What on earth had prompted that? His easy smile had changed, she noticed. It was as though he might resent Kane and Molly's display of togetherness. This man wore charm like a mask.

Underneath it, he might be as cutthroat as any pirate, for all she knew.

When the panic was over, Sienna sank back into her seat. She had a lot to think about. It sounded as though all four of them gathered around the table might have something to hide. She wondered all through dessert. Her friend Molly was desperate to know what Garett was concealing. Sienna was curious about him, too. If this international troubleshooter could be persuaded to audit her estate, it might do them both some good. While he checked her land and holdings, she would have a golden opportunity to find out his secrets by observing him.

Which she would do—with very great care.

It was still dark when Sienna woke next morning. She lay in bed, listening to owls calling in the wood as they made their way to bed. She loved this shadowy margin between night and day. Sleep left her refreshed, but there was still time to linger before the busy day crowded in. She stretched, wondering what Kane and Molly's visitor was doing now.

In order to change and still get home at a reasonable time for someone who had just been 'out for a walk' Sienna had left the dinner party straight after dessert. She remembered her last sight of Garett Lazlo with a pang. Her memory combined passion and panic, and she ran her hands over her naked skin as though she could still feel the sear of his gaze. He had stood up when she left, like a true gentleman, although the look in his eyes had been anything but good-mannered. I'll bet he only pretends to like me, Sienna thought. Whenever Kane had tried to press him into helping untangle her affairs, Garett had become lukewarm about the whole thing. His behaviour should have made Sienna glad that, if he did not accept the challenge to look over her estate she might never meet him again. Instead it left her feeling cheated, as though there was unfinished business between them.

Sienna knew this was a one-sided sensation. Garett Lazlo did not strike her as a man who would waste a single second worrying about *her*. As soon as the door had closed behind her last night he would have sunk straight back into his comfortable club chair beside the fire. Sienna idly imagined what might have happened next. No doubt Garett and Kane would have sampled the Bradleys' collection of fine wines until late into the night. Then Garett would have made his way up the villa's long marble staircase, perhaps stripping off that smart black silk tie as he went. He might even have been given the same guest suite Sienna had used when the Bradleys gave her refuge immediately after Aldo's death. She closed her eyes, remembering the comforting luxury of slipping between those crisp, freshly ironed cotton sheets. Now that tall American with the mysterious eyes was stretched out there instead. She wondered what he was wearing now—or what any single man wore in bed, for that matter.

Sienna had only ever slept with her husband.

The memory of Aldo made her shiver, and she turned over, burrowing down beneath the duvet in search of a warmth that was missing from her life. Aldo would never have moved as quickly as Garett had done to help her blot the spilled wine from Molly's tablecloth. Aldo would never have moved at all. In fact, he would have withered Sienna with a look if she had done anything to help the butler clean up. Silent rage would have radiated from him, spoiling the rest of the dinner party.

Presumably Garett Lazlo hid his true feelings in front of his friends. He had been light, easy company the night before. But there had been a few moments when she'd seen beneath the surface. She smiled, filling the shadowy dawn. Garett was obviously someone who liked being the centre of attention and totally in control. For a few glorious minutes she fantasised about him taking charge of her life. He would brush away all the petty worries and major concerns that loomed over her every waking moment. Sweeping her up in his arms, he would crush her tightly against his broad chest, kiss her until she lost her mind, and then—

And then the alarm burst into life, and Sienna had to drag on the harness of duty all over again.

The first thing she did was to inspect her evening dress as it hung on the front of her wardrobe. She would sponge it later. In the old days it would have been whisked away as soon as she'd stepped out of it. Sienna would not have concerned herself with trivial day-to-day matters like getting the gown all the way to the dry-cleaners in town and then fetching it again a few days later.

But these were not the old days, despite her stepmother's grand plans and secret schemes. Aldo was gone, and with him most of the money. Only Sienna's careful housekeeping managed to keep the bailiffs from the doors nowadays.

She thought over her most pressing problems as she showered and got ready for the day. This house, which some might say was her greatest financial asset, was also the biggest drain on her resources. It held no emotional pull for Sienna. She would have sold it in an instant, and gladly gone back to live in the little house where she had been born, but Imelda was convinced that no one would look at them twice if they left the villa.

Sienna sighed, brushing her long auburn hair in front of the bathroom mirror. It felt ungrateful to worry, somehow. Many people would kill to have problems like hers. Her father had worked hard to secure himself a respected position in the village. Signor Basso had owned the local mill and bakery, which at one time had brought in a good living. Unfortunately, after the death of Sienna's mother, her father had spent all his time on his business. He had never found any opportunity to benefit from his money. When his health had broken, Sienna had blackmailed him into taking a holiday on the Riviera dei Fiori to recover. While she had worked to keep his business going, her father had fallen prey to one of the women who haunted the coastal resorts looking for prosperous husbands. He had returned with Imelda as his wife, and an overdraft.

Signor Basso had started going downhill after that. He had died from overwork. Now his bakery and mill were empty and desolate. Imelda wanted the buildings sold, but Sienna kept trying to dodge the issue. They had been her home, and she loved them. She avoided her stepmother as much as possible. This was easy, as Imelda Basso spent virtually all her time in her self-contained suite of rooms on the villa's top floor. After engineering Sienna's marriage to the oldest euro millionaire in the province, Imelda was not going to give up the benefits of her new life easily.

As she left her own high-ceilinged rooms and walked out onto the upper landing, Sienna began to see her stepmother's point. This was a beautiful house, fading gracefully into old age. The cornices and chandeliers that had echoed with grand balls between the two World Wars were now dusty and dull. Such a house did not deserve to sink into its foundations, but restoring it was beyond Sienna. She walked downstairs and through to the kitchens, despairing all the way that the marble floors would never again ring to the clatter of footsteps or resonate with children's laughter. This old place deserved more. It wanted someone with enough money to treat it properly— like an aristocratic old lady with nothing to prove.

Sienna gave a sad smile as she reached for her apron. It hung on one of a row of curled brass hooks, left behind from the days when the house had employed dozens of staff. Even the servants' working quarters here were on an impressive scale. The parts that nobody of quality would dream of visiting had soaring ceilings and carved plaster-work. It was a shame those times were gone, but their passing gave Sienna one small freedom. She could at least work in her own kitchens. She much preferred keeping busy. She took pride in her cooking, as she did with her knitting. Making things with her own hands gave her a real sense of satisfaction.

Today would be a baking day, she decided. As well as bread and cakes, she would make enough pasta to last the week.

Starting before sunrise gave her a head start, but it was not all work. Each time she needed to use the sink, she paused to watch the sky over the nearest ridge of hills. First the pearly shades of morning became suffused with rose-pink, aqua, and finally the purest shade of Madonna blue.

It was a sight that warmed her heart. No matter how busy she was, Sienna always made time to marvel and dream.

Today was slightly different. From the start, she tried to keep her fantasies to a minimum, because they kept being hijacked by thoughts of Garett Lazlo. Each time she took her mind off the task in hand it wandered back to the previous day—and night. He had disrupted her work at the market, and then distracted her over dinner. She could not afford to let him wreck another day. Turning back to the big marble slab she used for working dough, she scooped great measures of flour onto its grey-veined surface. Hollowing out its peak, she broke egg after egg into the Vesuvius-like caldera. Completely absorbed, she did not hear footsteps approaching the open kitchen door.

'Good morning.'

Sienna turned, amazed. Her darkest, most private thoughts had sprung to life in the very real and very dashing form of Garett Lazlo. He had one palm resting against the doorframe, while his other hand was hooked into the belt of his well-cut jeans. All her feverish ideas of him languishing in bed vanished in an instant. He definitely did not look like a man who had been drinking late into the night. His white short-sleeved polo shirt showed off muscular arms and a temptation of chest hair at its open neck. The thoroughly civilised tuxedo he had worn for dinner the night before had aroused Sienna without hinting at any of the wonders it was hiding. Now she was faced with 'Garett Casual', it took her some seconds to find her voice.

'Mr Lazlo…I never expected to see you again so soon…' She managed eventually.

'Likewise—but I never could resist anything that Molly asked of me, and she's determined to get you sorted out. So, against my better judgement, I've come over to make you a proposition.'

He strolled into the kitchen, gazing up at its high ceilings.

Sienna did not need to copy him. She knew what he was looking at, and it hit her like a physical pain.

'Don't—please don't…' she pleaded. 'I haven't had a chance to get the cobwebs down for ages…'

He lowered his gaze to hers.

'Surely your staff worry about all that, not you?'

'I—I don't have any proper staff. I have to do most of the work myself…although, as you can see, an awful lot of it has to stay undone. Like cleaning the ceilings,' she finished miserably.

He grimaced, and turned his attention to the dough she was working on. Its clinging strands had such a good hold on Sienna that she had no hope of a quick escape from her visitor's scrutiny.

'Don't bother dusting on my account, *signora*. It's too late for that. You'll only get bits in your cooking. What are you making?'

'I've got several things in progress at the moment. There was a nice fresh batch of candied peel in Piccia market the other day. When I saw it, and remembered how long it was since I last tasted *pandolce*, I just had to buy some,' she said breathlessly, nodding towards the kitchen dresser.

Garett went over to it. For once he was in no particular hurry to get down to business, so this was a good diversion. Hollow shells of lemon, orange and citron peel crusted with sugar lay on a lake of crinkled cellophane. He bent down and considered them like an expert.

'When I was little, I always used to wonder about sugarplums whenever some do-gooder read us the poem that starts "'Twas the night before Christmas…" but none of us kids had ever seen one. Are they like this, *signora*?'

'I have no idea.'

He broke off a fragment of sweet orange rind and popped it into his mouth.

'That,' he said with relish, 'is even better than I imagined it would be.'

'They always say that forbidden fruits taste sweetest.'

It was then that he saw the look on Sienna's face.

'You tipped your head toward them,' he said, in his own defence. 'So I thought you were giving me the go-ahead, since you were up to your elbows over there. No matter— I'll replace it when I next take you out to lunch.'

Sienna stopped kneading. A trickle of egg breached the defence of flour between her hands. She didn't notice.

'Lunch again? With you? Me?'

'Yes,' he said confidently, as though there might be some problem with the translation.

'But…Mr Lazlo—you don't know what you're saying! Whatever has come over you? I can't be seen in public with a lone man a second time. Especially not the *same* lone man. It's bad enough that you have invited yourself into my kitchen this morning. What will everybody think? What will my stepmother say?'

'Why should *you* care about that?' he chuckled.

Sienna could not believe what she was hearing. The single meander of reckless egg that had escaped from her dough split into a delta and dribbled across the tabletop, heading for the floor. Cooking was the last thing on her mind now. Incredulous, she stared at him. 'Because—because…'

He waited. Garett was not normally a patient man, but he was almost enjoying this.

'Mmm?'

Sienna stopped trying to find the words everyone else wanted her to say, and went back to the wreckage of her dough. The soggy mountain of its remains was like her life. It was formless, hopeless, and a bit wet. Hot with indignation, she began furiously recapturing the escaped egg by sweeping flour around the heap to enfold it all again.

He watched her for some time before speaking.

'Suit yourself, *signora*—although lunch is nothing compared to what else I might have on offer. I've come to you with a business proposition.'

Long practice had taught Garett Lazlo exactly how to deal with women. Lowering his chin and raising his dark brows, he coaxed a response from her with an expression full of promise. It worked instantly.

'Go on, *signor*,' she said, with a nervousness in her voice that she tried to disguise.

He leant casually against the worktop. 'I think a lot of the Bradleys, and they're worried about you. They want me to help you. Last night I told them over and over again, in words of one syllable, that I've come here for a holiday, not to work. But nothing I could do would stop them nagging, so in the end I had to override my better judgement and give in.' He smiled in a way that he knew no woman was able to resist. 'So here's my offer: I will bring all my expertise to your house and estate, but for a very limited period only. This place is going to be put straight in the shortest possible time. Then I'm out of here. What you do with it then is up to you. I told you yesterday that you should grab every opportunity to make your dreams come true. So when I've finished you can sell everything and go wild with the cash, or carry my business plan forward, or simply leave all my good works to crumble into dust. It will be entirely up to you.'

He spoke in a low, persuasive whisper. It was charming, it was warm, and when Sienna shivered it wasn't his clinical businessman's brain that was affecting her.

'But a successful man like you isn't running a charity.' she said uncertainly. 'What is all this going to cost me?'

'Genius has its price, of course, but it won't be anything that you can't afford.'

'Which is?'

His lips parted. Sienna caught sight of the gleam of his perfect white teeth.

One way or another, this meant trouble.

CHAPTER FIVE

'Is THERE somewhere we can talk frankly, Signora di Imperia, without the risk of being disturbed? Or coated in flour.' He looked down at her hands meaningfully.

'Of course—give me a few minutes to settle my step-mother. I shall tell her Molly has arrived here for another lace-making lesson. That will keep her well out of the way. Then I will make us both some coffee—'

'No—don't bother to do that, *signora*. I've brought something with me that will take its place. And I'll sort everything out down here.'

Sienna washed her hands, and then ran upstairs. It took her a few minutes and a lot of half-truths to settle Imelda. Struggling with her conscience would take Sienna much longer. By the time she reached the kitchen again she was pink with guilt. Her colour deepened when she found that Garett had been roaming around the ground floor unsupervised. He was waiting for her in the only place fit for visitors. She dreaded to think what he might have come across before he found it.

Her guest stood in the drawing room, beside its central table. The salon was large, and flooded with natural sunlight. With his back to one of the tall windows he made a forbidding silhouette. When he turned to face her Sienna realised he was in the midst of opening a bottle of champagne. The cork was released with a sigh, and he poured out two crystal flutes before placing the bottle down on a silver tray. The room was so quiet as he picked up one of the glasses and walked towards Sienna that she could hear its foam of bubbles bursting at the brim.

'Don't bother saying it's too early for this until you've heard everything I have to say,' he murmured.

She tried to refuse, but he stood his ground.

'One glass of bubbles *signora*. Allow yourself a little luxury,' he said mildly, offering her the glass.

She eyed it warily. 'I have told you how difficult things are in Piccia, *signor*. If anyone saw you coming in here with that bottle, or if they discovered that I have been alone in this salon with you…' She wavered, and his face immediately became strained.

'Signora di Imperia—Sienna—you can't go on tying yourself up in other people's morals. If you don't have the spirit to act in your own best interests, then you might as well simply hand the keys of this place to the nearest bank manager and save yourself, Molly and Kane a lot of—'

'I *do* have spirit.' Sienna tilted her chin. She had cut him off in mid-flow, and his eyes flashed a warning. She took no notice—but she did take the champagne.

'It is simply that I must respect the wishes of my step-mother, *signor*,' Sienna said with regret. 'She is not strong. The dignity of my father's name and my late husband's house are the only things she has left in life. I must respect that, and be respected in return.'

'I heard less favourable comments about Imelda from Molly.'

Sienna took a sip of champagne before replying. Lowering the glass, she gave him a frank, open look.

'You will never hear them from my lips, Mr Lazlo. And that is why warning my stepmother that Molly is visiting makes sure she stays up in her suite. Molly and Imelda have met on several occasions.'

'Crossed swords, you mean?'

Sienna took another sip of champagne.

'I've never tasted anything like this before. I want to enjoy it.'

'You can.' A girl like you should, he thought, moving in to refill her glass. 'There's plenty more where this came from. My business has been running on it for more than twenty years.'

Sienna accepted a top-up, but on her own terms. 'I must warn you, Mr Lazlo. I have no intention of getting drunk so that you can take advantage of me.'

He met her stare with interest, and tried his hardest to conceal a smile. 'I'm shocked that you should think so little of me, *signora*. I don't need alcohol to help me seduce a woman. Good grief—what sort of men have you been used to?'

None except Aldo, Sienna thought. And he was certainly *nothing* like you, Garett Lazlo.

She took another small sample of the champagne—her courage increasing.

'The only men I deal with are those who can be useful to me.'

She heard herself marking out terms, and hoped her

amazement did not show in her face. I sounded almost snappy, she thought. Where did *that* come from? Champagne at this time in the morning obviously has its uses.

'Then we speak the same language, Signora di Imperia.' He inclined his head graciously. 'That is exactly my offer. I can be everything you need.'

His expression was impenetrable. Sienna waited for him to explain, growing uneasier by the second. Finally, her resistance crumbled.

'Please come to the point, Mr Lazlo.'

'Only when we become Garett and Sienna again. You were happy enough with that informality last night.'

'I'd rather keep things formal while we're alone. Please—if you don't mind.'

Sienna netted the fingers of both her hands around her champagne flute to give her courage. 'Look, Signor Lazlo—Garett—it won't be long before my stepmother is calling for her lunch tray…'

'Then she must learn that her beautiful, attentive nurse has a life of her own, *signora*.'

His eyes temporarily lost their direct, piercing look. Now his expression was softer—but probably more dangerous, Sienna realised.

She was right. Reaching out, he took the glass from her fingers. As her hands dropped to her sides he caught one and drew her closer to the table. His fingers fastened firmly on her wrist, expecting resistance. When she allowed herself to be led in silence, he smiled appreciatively. This was more like it. In the hours since she'd left the Bradleys' dinner party Garett had spent a long time savouring all the feelings she aroused in him. They did not affect his determination to resist her. In fact they strengthened his resolve. Fantasies were so much easier to manipulate than real life. All his affairs with rich, powerful women had been turbulent and irritating. A stress-free, hands-off approach would make a pleasant change.

Sienna might have a thread of steel, but it was deeply buried. The nervousness shadowing her eyes proved that. Garett wondered how long he could extend the pleasure of imagining that pliant little beauty submitting to him. The fantasy was a long way removed from reality, of course. Her nervousness and his determination to resist would see to that.

His smile darkened. Anticipation was the greatest aphrodisiac, and it was working its magic on him right now.

'What is the matter, Mr Lazlo?'

She was pulling away from him. He let her go—but slowly, enjoying the sensation of dragging his fingers lightly over her skin.

Sienna enjoyed it, too, which was why she did not retreat too quickly. Decency was not what filled her mind now. He was touching her. His hand was warm and welcoming, a world away from Aldo's cold desiccation. What would it feel like to abandon all her principles and surrender to that slow-burning passion in his eyes?

'I'm afraid you aren't going to like what I have to say.' He sighed.

If only that was true, Sienna thought, slowly lowering her lashes. It was a gesture that disappointed them both. She wanted to go on looking at him; he wanted her to.

'It might be better if you got out of this place right now, *signora*. Turn your back and walk away while you still have everything going for you. With youth on your side you can go anywhere, do anything, be anyone. If you stay chained to life in this place as it is, it will be your financial death sentence.'

The quiet confidence behind his words was powerful. If she was being honest with herself, Sienna had suspected the truth behind his words all along. But this was a man who had everything: all the calm assurance and determination she lacked. It was all very well for *him* to suggest that she should tear her life up by the roots and transplant it somewhere else on a whim…

She steeled herself to challenge him. 'What proof do you have for saying that?'

A shadow passed across his expression. Sienna had managed to surprise him. It gave her an unexpected shot of pleasure.

He shook his head gravely. 'I was up before first light to check out what the Bradleys were letting me in for. Unfortunately, what little I've seen of your estate has already opened my eyes to the difficulties of living around here. Unless you can get your act together right now, *signora*, your estate is going to be consumed by the starving Italian earth—and sooner rather than later.'

He took a long, slow drink of champagne while she registered his warning.

'Do you have any qualifications which allow you to be so certain about that?' She spoke slowly. Her mind was working on automatic. She was already fully aware of the qualifications he possessed for turning her mind and body into quivering jelly.

'Absolutely none—beyond my total honesty,' he said frankly. 'The point is, *signora*, I don't have to be a world authority on Ligurian farming to see that your place is going down the pan. Fences allowed to rot, the wilderness encroaching on your beautiful threadbare old villa as though it was Sleeping Beauty's palace—' He stopped.

Sienna immediately filled his pause with fantasy. He was Prince Charming, riding up on his white stallion to save her. If only…

After a long pause, she sighed. 'I suppose you must be right. There are times when I feel as if I am sleepwalking through life. The harder I try, the more difficult it is to please everybody.' She put a hand up to cover her face, desolate. The tiny sound of a glass being put down on the tray cut through her absorption. Before she could be alarmed, a firm hand was sliding around her shoulders

'You are your own woman,' Garett said gently. 'It should never be a case of denying yourself a chance of happiness just because of what others might think.'

Wordlessly, she looked up into his face. His jaw was as resolute as ever, but when those unfathomable eyes looked at her now there was a glitter of something recognisable deep within them. She had first seen that look last night, when she'd walked into the Bradleys' dining room.

With a shiver, she tried to withdraw from his touch. Garett was having none of it. He might be determined not to seduce her, but he had never been able to resist playing with fire.

'Let's put that theory to the test, shall we?' His fingers ran around the gentle curve of her chin. His fantasies were calling for some real fuel. Suddenly hot and hard, he closed in on her body. 'You are as vital a creature as I am, Sienna di Imperia. Why do you try and hide it?' he breathed, soft and low.

'I—I don't know what you are talking about…'

'Innocence isn't the real reason your eyes refuse to meet mine, is it? No—it is quite the opposite. The reason for your rigid refusal to loosen up and enjoy the party last night is because you and I both know the truth. You want me. It is as simple as that. I'm guessing that for the first time in your life you have identified something you want so much that it might make you turn and swim against the tide of public opinion. Well, here's something that will convince you that your life shouldn't begin and end with other people.'

His hands slipped around her narrow waist. Sienna was transfixed. She knew she ought to call for help—scream, or make a scene—anything to contrast her decency with his lust. That would be the right and proper thing to do. But Garett's fingers were pressing against the thin cotton of her sundress. She could feel their warmth. Humanity was something that had been missing from her life for so long, and she could not bear to deny herself any longer.

'Someone might see.' Her words drifted between them as though through a dream, and Sienna realised she must have spoken them.

'Who? You've already told me you don't have any staff.'

She felt his words rise up from deep within his chest to chuckle into her hair.

'No, but Signora Mortari comes to help with the cooking on Fridays, and there's Ermanno and his wife, who run the home farm—'

'Today isn't Friday. And farming business doesn't include looking through your drawing room windows, does it?'

Within the circle of his arms, Sienna trembled.

'I could go straight over to that door and escape.' She tried to convince herself.

'Of course you could—if you thought anything bad was going to happen.'

His expression was that of a leopard appreciating his prey. He had not moved since laying claim to her with his hands, but now the smile that had been playing over his lips faded.

'But it isn't, is it?' Sienna said, and then cursed herself silently. She had meant it as a statement. What if he heard it as a challenge? She leaned back slightly against his grip, still trying to keep a decent distance between them.

'That rather depends how you define the word "bad".'

His voice was as smooth as silk. When he let her go, Sienna almost regretted it. Picking up her glass of champagne again, he poured into it another cascade of foam before handing it over. Then he raised his own glass, scrutinising the lines of tiny bubbles fizzing up to the golden surface. His dark, intelligent eyes watched her over the rim of his glass as he took a long, slow draught of the fine wine.

'I'm a man who always gets what he wants. And the one thing that connects all the things I want is success.'

Sienna trembled. In an effort to hide her nervousness, she gripped the slender cylinder of her glass. His eyes darted to the tiny movement, and he smiled. Too late, she realised her knuckles must have bleached with the pressure, betraying her fear.

Garett was in no hurry. There was absolutely no point. He could have her—at any time and in any place. It had been obvious from the look in her eyes on that first day, down in the marketplace, but taking her was the *last* thing he wanted. Her fragile state combined with this wreck of a house made Sienna di Imperia a challenge too far.

But he needed to silence Molly's nagging—and his own conscience. It had taken some thought, but he had worked out how to do it. The satisfaction of knowing broadened his smile.

'I can see that you are desperate to know what I am talking about, *signora*.'

'I suppose…' Sienna swallowed hard, trying to keep the sad inevitability out of her voice. 'I suppose you are going to suggest something indecent?'

CHAPTER SIX

HE LAUGHED softly. The echo reflected around the shabby surfaces of the gold and crystal salon.

'Well, that rather depends on how you interpret the word, Signora di Imperia. Kane and Molly ought to have more sense, but I believe they expect me to succumb to your pretty face and make everything all right. Though, let's face it, I'm more likely to make you a straight offer to buy your wreck of an estate than I am to fall in love with you.'

He laughed. Sienna joined in, but only because she was desperate to appear polite. In reality she felt crushed and confused.

'Let me put it to you straight: Kane and Molly suspect your life is in chaos. If you carry on firefighting as you have been doing—patching here, recycling there—any money you currently have will trickle away completely. What this place needs is one massive, carefully planned overhaul to give it an independent future. You are already being run ragged by your stepmother, or so I'm told. Unless you come up with the goods, *signora*, she won't rest until she sees you safely married again. If you won't take my advice and get out while you still can, the obvious solution to all these challenges is simple. Get your estate and buildings up and running properly, so they can support you. Then you can thumb your nose at them all and live the way *you* want to. It will take money—a lot of it. But if you are willing to do as I want, then I'll finance everything until this old place can fund a mortgage to repay me. Then you can grab your dream—whatever it may be.' He stopped, and his smile broadened.

Here it comes, thought Sienna bleakly.

He took a long slow drink of his champagne. Sienna watched him with an awful feeling of inevitability. He looked like a tiger quaffing cream.

She sighed. He might as well not have bothered with the champagne, the smiles, and the artful pauses. All her adult life her body had been sold—she knew nothing else. First it had been Aldo, now it was the horrible prospect of marriage to grisly cousin Claudio.

'You mean…you and I…' Her voice faltered and died. Garett's flirtation, her fantasies, the brush of his fingers against her skin—sex would ruin all that, dragging it through the mire and rubbing all the nap off her dreams. She swallowed hard. 'You…and…I…'

However often she repeated it, she could not get any further. The words lodged in her throat. She could not bear to put into words the hideous reality that it must become.

His voice broke over her misery. '*Signora*—I offer all my skills. But I will want something in return.'

Sienna could not move. She was staring at the floor, knowing that Imelda would scream at her to look him straight in the face and thank her good fortune. This was, after all, a man who had all the good-looks and charm any woman could ever want. According to her friend Molly, he had the money too. Everything about Garett Lazlo should have been so right. In her dreams last night Sienna had fallen into his arms a thousand times. But in the full glare of daylight life was turning out to be as hard and cruel and painful as always. Aldo's death had dropped a heavy burden on her. Now she was being offered paradise—but at an enormous cost.

Not that she should have expected anything better. Shouldn't Garett's opening statement have trampled all her fantasies about a white knight riding to her rescue? *I'm more likely to make you a straight offer to buy your wreck of an estate than I am to fall in love with you!* he had said. There had been more feeling in that statement than in any other. It was a trait Sienna recognised. And the easy way he spoke about her wanting him. She shut her eyes and thought back to her late husband, Aldo.

Hadn't her marriage to him been arranged on exactly the same lines? The old man had been invited to dine by Imelda, who had been playing the part of lonely widow at the time. She'd been looking for advice about what to do with the Basso property in the village, she'd said.

Aldo di Imperia had been quick to spot an opportunity to expand his small empire. And then Sienna had opened the front door of the home she shared with her stepmother. She had seen a stooped husk of a man, bearing roses. He had seen an opportunity.

The Widow Basso had got his advice, but Sienna had been given the flowers. And so it had begun...

She needed time to think.

'As I see it, Signor Lazlo, I can either economise still further, or get a job,' she said slowly. 'On the one hand, I can't believe it's possible to cut any more corners. I've scrimped and scraped for so long I don't think I know how to spend any longer. On the other hand there are no jobs in Piccia beyond the co-operative. The few euros that my work brings in could never support Imelda and me.'

'Then dump her and save yourself.'

'No. I can never do that, *signor*. I made a promise to my father that I would care for her. I shall have to manage.'

'I am offering you an escape route,' he repeated, as though either of them needed a reminder. 'Why go on starving in a ruin, heckled by the original wicked stepmother?'

'Please don't insult my family, *signor*,' Sienna said in a small voice. She had to be polite, but that did not mean she had to let him get away with murder—just something worse.

'Imelda Basso is not your family. She is merely a woman with an eye for the main chance.'

Sienna heard him tap his glass, and then he began pacing to and fro in front of her. She could see the gloss on his handmade leather shoes, but she could not and would not raise her head to see his expression.

'Molly says you own a little place in the centre of the village. Is that right?'

'It's the place where I was born, yes,' Sienna said miserably. If only she could be there now, safe and sound. But Imelda insisted she stayed at the villa, to keep her company. Sienna never had time to visit her old family home at the bakery now. She was always so busy—running around doing farm work, cooking, working for the co-operative or beating back the undergrowth around the villa.

'If you are so determined not to sell up, perhaps you could renovate your old home first? When that's finished, you can move back in, leaving Imelda here. Once everything is up and running, operating this estate according to my guidelines will free you financially. If you're determined, there's profit to be made here—with plenty left over to pay someone to run around after your stepmother. That will please her, and rescue you into the bargain. Better that than waiting around like a parcel to be haggled over by any interested party.'

'When I married Aldo I became a part of his family's history. It is my duty to keep his house and his memory free from scandal.'

'But you won't be able to do any of that without a secure investment base.'

Suddenly his feet disappeared from Sienna's field of vision.

'Oh, *damn* your stubbornness!'

Sienna jumped, and looked up at him in alarm. The only person who ever spoke to her like that was Imelda. For seconds on end she stared at Garett's broad back. 'When do you want me?' Her words whispered out, with hardly the strength to cross the space between them.

The moment she spoke he caught her eye and held it, exactly as he had done in the market. But this time it was different. This time she was scared. She had looked up expecting to find that his face was cold and calculating— except that it wasn't. She blinked. For a split second she thought she saw confusion there, but no—when she looked again his expression was totally unreadable.

'What did you say?'

She wavered. Speaking the words had been hard enough. Repeating them would be torture. She tried to make the awful task easier. Garett was young and gorgeous—but to sleep with a man for gain was still nothing short of prostitution. Yet her situation was desperate—no money, no hope, no future—so didn't she owe it to herself to grab this one chance? She knew better than to expect any happiness from her life. The fact that Garett Lazlo could make such a suggestion must mean he was no better than any other man, but she would have to close her mind to that. She had managed to shut out a lot of pain and disappointment over the years in that way. Her experience with Garett would be familiar in that respect. But, despite his lack of heart, surely he possessed all the other qualifications she needed? Sienna knew that from the way his every movement fired such unusual sensations in her body. Garett was a towering monument to fantasy. His clear skin, the direct dark brown stare, and those strong, square hands...

'All right, then. I'll sleep with you,' she said quietly.

'What?'

The beginnings of the smile on his face froze into a fixed stare. He seemed to be having difficulty in understanding her reply. Sienna was not surprised. Her throat was so constricted the words had hardly been able to struggle out.

'Yes,' she managed, with more conviction this time. 'I accept. If you can rescue my future, then I will spend one night with you.'

He did not answer for a long time. His mind was too full. He had never in his life met a woman like Sienna di Imperia. First she ran away from him in a five-star restaurant. Now she invited herself into his bed. But, being the girl she was, Sienna was not coiling herself around him like a career courtesan. Oh, no. She was approaching him like an appointment with danger.

Looking into her eyes—when she actually managed to meet his gaze—banished any feelings of anger or offence he might have had. It didn't take a financial wizard to realise that her marriage of convenience had taken a heavy toll. For once in his life he was lost for words. There really did not seem to be anything he could say without sounding patronising. If he did that, she might cry. Then he would have to put his arms around her, and all hell would probably break loose.

Perplexed, Garett stuck one hand in his pocket. There he felt the cold kiss of coins, and it gave him an idea. Money really could talk—so it was lucky he was such a good conversationalist. He had spent years thinking on his feet. With relief, he found he could still do it, despite all the circumstances.

'Well, well, well—you're a dark horse and no mistake, aren't you, *signora*?' he breathed.

He was playing for time, but she showed no signs of realising that. She was gorgeous, and twenty-four hours before he would have seduced her like a shot if it hadn't been for his mad idea of taking a holiday from life. Now she was offering herself to him like a sacrifice. He grimaced. Her attitude was turning something he had always treated as an amusement into a dark, hole-and-corner obscenity. That was not his style at all.

He knew she must be afraid of what he might say now. She was certainly far too nervous to look at him. Their relationship had changed—and not in a good way. She had been a fantasy. He didn't want to force her to live his dream. Why had he got into this mess, and what in the hell had persuaded her to agree? He had never paid a woman to sleep with him before—and wasn't that what this amounted to? The stark reality of it hit him hard. Even after decent champagne, she clearly had no stomach for sex. She was as rigid as ever—and now there was genuine fear in her eyes. Garett had never backed down on a deal in his life. Nor had he ever refused to rise to a challenge. And he was not about to start now.

'My undertaking is to put in place a complete and thorough restoration of your house and estate,' he announced. 'In return for one night together when the work has been done.'

That gave him an automatic get-out clause, but with luck she would not realise it. Garett had exacting standards. The international business world was bound to track him down and reclaim him before he was satisfied that her project was finished. He would leave without taking Sienna up on her offer. With a sigh of relief he would be out of her life for ever, with no loss of face on either side. She would never need to present herself like a trembling lamb on his altar. He had no idea where she had picked up the notion that his fee was her body, but now that she had suggested it he was going to make the best of the situation. Neither of them could retreat now without a total loss of dignity and self-esteem. And Sienna doesn't have much of either, Garett thought with a strange pang. That must be why she came up with the notion—she has absolutely nothing to lose. If it had not been so tragic he might have laughed. Unlike her, he was supposed to possess all the chips in life's poker game. Yet right now he felt as miserable as she looked.

'*Signora*, let's have a toast!'

His voice was as light and teasing as ever. Warily, Sienna looked him up and down. She was considering all her fantasies, every word they had shared over the past twenty-four hours. Garett was totally irresistible—in the same way that a spring avalanche carried all before it. I can always claim I'm being picked up and bundled along by events beyond my control as usual, she thought tentatively. At least this time it will be with a truly desirable man. But one who has secrets, she reminded herself with a shiver.

Slowly, hesitantly, she raised her glass and let him kiss it with his own. The fine lead crystal chimed, and it was over. Her fate was sealed.

'You can rely on me, *signora*,' Garett was saying. 'I will not lay a single finger on you until work here is finished to our complete satisfaction. My self-restraint is about to become legendary.'

He took the champagne bottle over to the French doors. Forcing open the rusted catch, he gave one last lingering look at its label. Then he watered the overgrown flowerbed with the remaining contents. Sienna watched in silent acceptance of the waste. Garett shut out the fragrance of wine-soaked rosemary. Then he gestured towards the silver tray and its abandoned glasses. 'You take care of those while I dispose of the evidence. I delayed your cooking. You had better get back to it.'

He strode out of the room. By the time Sienna reached the kitchen sink he was returning from the yard empty-handed.

All her previous spirit had evaporated, he noticed with a twist of distaste.

'Don't look like that, *signora*. Many women find sleeping in my bed a pleasure.'

'I'm not too grand to starve in a wreck like this.' Sienna's reply was heavy. 'And it isn't the sleeping that worries me.'

He exhaled sharply and planted his hands on his hips. 'Look, *signora*, forget about all that for the moment. I've got much more important things than sex on my mind right now. I should be making a start on managing your project!'

Sienna eyed him cautiously. The restless air about him was constant, but it was no longer directed at her. He clearly had other targets in his sights. It made her feel less like a hunting trophy and more like an abandoned parcel— something to be worked around, or tripped over and cursed at at regular intervals. It was a role Sienna was used to. Sex might be a physical torment for her, but pandering to others was something she could manage *very* well.

'Of course.' She said meekly. 'What do you want me to do first?'

He glanced around, a hawk on the lookout.

'Er…you can finish your baking, and then get cleared up in here. That's all.'

'I could help you outside,' she ventured uncertainly.

'No. Your place is here in the house—at least for the moment. I make better headway when I work alone.'

He was watching her as though his mind was operating at a much deeper level than his words. He saw Sienna's shoulder muscles begin to soften. There was the slightest slowing in her movements as she tied on her apron again. His plan was taking effect—for the moment at least. She no longer saw him as an immediate threat. That suited him. With a crooked smile, he seasoned his story with some diffidence.

'The truth is I can't wait to get back to my office job. And I'd *really* hate to have all the other billionaires laughing at me because I had to abandon my holiday project,' he joked, in an attempt to make light of the situation. 'I can hardly set myself up to advise clients if I leave my own work half finished, can I?'

She looked up, and this time she gave him a sad smile.

He knew then that there was hope for her. There was still a spark of something left. All it needed was encouragement. She stopped assaulting the dough she was working with, and began patting it instead.

'You've beaten that *pandolce* into a pulp, then?'

She shook her head. As she moved across the room to dampen a clean towel at the sink sunlight danced over her copper hair, making it shine like the array of pots and pans hanging from their rack above the kitchen table.

'This is pasta dough, *signor*. The cake is rising in a tin under that cloth over there on the dresser.'

'Pasta? I thought that came in tubs from Marshall's Deli, smothered in mayo.'

Sienna frowned, grazing her lower lip with her teeth as she covered the freshly finished dough to stop it drying out. 'Mayo?'

'Mayonnaise,' he translated helpfully.

'I must try that,' she murmured.

Garett laughed his tantalising laugh.

'Don't worry—you don't need to humour me, Signora di Imperia.'

'No—really—I like trying out new recipes. Aldo—

my late husband—knew what he liked, and unfortunately that didn't include many things. I cook all sorts of things now that I would never have dreamed of making a few months ago.'

'Imagine that—I've never had home-made pasta.' Garett shook his head slowly.

'Then you've never really tasted the best.' Sienna turned back one corner of the red and white checked cloth she had used to cover the dough and pulled off a handful of smooth, silky pasta in the raw. 'This is how it begins. Spaghetti, fusilli, manilli—it all starts out the same,' she went on, relaxing still further.

He was watching with genuine interest. The threat had receded for a little while, and Sienna was glad.

She warmed the dough for a moment, by rolling it between her hands, and then went back to the kitchen table. A pasta machine was clamped to one of its edges.

'Do you make pasta every day, *signora*?'

'I don't do all *this* every day, no. I prepare it in bulk once a week or so. We eat some fresh that day, and I dry the rest. It's easy enough, but it takes a long time to do it properly. And the trouble is, of course, that as the sheets of dough get thinner, they get longer, and end up draped all along the length of the table. That's why I like to make it early, when there is no one else around.'

'Would it be any easier with two?'

She looked at him quickly, but when her answer was not immediate he went over to the sink and washed his hands.

Sienna was impressed. After all these years, she *still* had to remind Signora Mortari to do that before handling food.

'You must do a lot of cooking, Mr Lazlo.'

'No—French toast is about my limit. But when I was a kid, they parked me in front of a television showing too many public information films. It put me off salmonella for life. Oh—and go back to calling me Garett.'

'Yes—Garett.'

He was ready for a towel. Before he could reach for the one draped over Sienna's shoulder, she flipped it across at him. As an attempt to keep him at arm's length, it failed miserably. Once he had dried his hands, he folded the towel in half lengthwise and dropped it onto her shoulder again. Sienna half turned her head, but stopped when it became obvious this was not some flirtatious gesture on his part. Although he took his time, it was only to drape the folds carefully.

'There.'

'Thank you,' Sienna muttered, edging away. She could not escape for long.

'What next?'

'Oh…'

Sienna knew she should act quickly, and brush off his offer of help, but it was impossible. The nearness of him was bringing back all the strange feelings of guilty pleasure she had experienced at Il Pettirosso.

'Well, Garett…if you stand next to me…' she said, keeping her head down. 'I have to feed the dough between these rollers…'

'It's like a mangle, squeezing the water out of wet washing.'

Sienna stopped and looked up at him uncertainly. 'Are you making fun of me?' she ventured. 'Are you going to say you've seen a mangle just like ours in a museum?'

'Not at all.' He frowned. 'We had one at home. When I was four years old I tried feeding a dead rat through it. Thirty years later I can still remember the noise my mother made when she saw it.'

Sienna exploded with laughter, then instantly clapped a hand to her mouth.

'You aren't telling me they have rats in America?'

'They do where I come from. Great big ones!' he added with relish when she gasped.

'I suppose it was left to your father to clear up the mess?' she giggled.

'No. He only ever came home when he wanted something.'

His reply silenced her. Sienna knew all about that sort of a relationship. Her stomach began to churn, so she moved quickly to fill the awkward silence between them. Setting the rollers of the pasta machine to their widest setting, she lodged one end of the dough between them. As she began feeding it through, Garett bent over her, intrigued by what was going on.

'So, although this looks like a complicated device, its design is actually quite simple?'

'Yes—you just keep feeding dough through it over and over again, each time narrowing the gap between the rollers so that the sheets become thinner and thinner.'

'And longer and longer—I can see why this job will be easier with two,' he mused, as the dough zigzagged into a neat stack beneath the bottom roller. 'How do you make it fold like that?'

Sienna glowed. She had actually managed to impress

somebody for once. She gave him an impish smile. 'It takes years of practice.'

He returned her look with equal mischief, and she had to confess.

'Not really—it just comes out like that automatically.'

'You don't say?'

He was already moving to take the handle from her, expecting her to stand back as if it was his divine right. Although his arrogance annoyed her, something stopped Sienna putting her feelings into words and she retreated in silence.

'There—look. I'm a natural.' He nodded towards the river of pasta that was falling in graceful folds onto the worktop.

'Careful—if you don't keep the underside of the machine clear the individual leaves stick together, and then there is no prising them apart.'

Sienna reached under the pasta machine exactly as Garett swept the handle around again. His knuckles struck the back of her hand and she leapt back in alarm.

He winced on her behalf. 'That must have hurt. Sorry. There wasn't much clearance between the table and my fist. Are you all right?'

'Yes—yes—it was just the shock that made me jump—'

'Let me see.'

He reached out and caught her wrist. His touch was light but firm. Sienna watched as he drew her hand towards him. It lay motionless in his grasp. She knew by now that there was no earthly point in trying to resist him. She tried to summon up all the fear she should feel at the prospect of paying him back for saving her home, but it was hopeless.

CHAPTER SEVEN

HE MUST have known what was going through her mind, because he levelled a dark stare straight at her.

'You are afraid I'm going to call in my debt early. Don't be. I've told you I'm not looking to do that.'

'If you say so,' Sienna said, sounding more confident than she felt.

'This is how it is going to be, Sienna. Until your house and estate are completely together again. I give you my word—and I never go back on that.'

His fingers were warm and confident on her skin as he gently turned her hand over in his.

'It was the back of my hand—not there.' Sienna felt bound to say it, but secretly she was glad when he took no notice and continued to study her pale, smooth palm.

'Ah, yes, but this is the point where I tell you about the glowing future I can see for the Entroterra estate, outlined here in your hand.'

'The pasta will dry up.'

'And that's exactly what I see here.'

Flirting with beautiful girls was a difficult habit for him

to break, he thought wryly. He scraped a tiny flake of desiccated dough from her skin.

'Lucky in love, unlucky in lunch.'

Sienna pulled her hand away sharply. 'There won't *be* any lunch if I don't get on with this,' she said hurriedly, desperate to turn away from his provocative gaze. 'I'll turn the handle this time, and you can support the dough when it comes out from between the rollers. If you don't mind,' she added shyly.

They worked in silence as the mobile creamy pasta was cranked through, centimetre by centimetre. After the first run Sienna adjusted the rollers and sent the sheet through a second time. As the process was repeated over and again the dough grew longer and thinner, forced through a narrower and narrower gap in the machine.

'This is making me feel hungry,' Garett said, when the dough began to emerge through the narrowest setting. The pasta was so thin now that it would have been possible to read newsprint through it. He held part of it up to the light, marvelling at its texture. 'It makes me wish I hadn't skipped breakfast.'

Sienna looked at him incredulously. 'How can anyone manage to leave the house without food?'

'Eating first thing in the morning slows me up. Missing breakfast means I can be on the spot and busy before anyone else. It makes extra time to fit in more work. But…if you're so concerned, maybe you'd like to try and find me something?'

It was the sort of order Sienna was only too happy to follow. She went over to where the *pandolce* was rising. Lifting one corner of the brightly coloured teatowel covering it, she frowned. 'This will take some time, but I could make you some stracchi with pesto instead.'

'Whatever it is, if it plugs a gap fast, I'll try it.'

She had been starting to come out of her shell again, but with that remark he saw her contract slightly.

'I'm sure it'll be delicious, Sienna. What is it, by the way?'

'Stracchi are thin sheets of pasta. Pesto is made from toasted pinenuts ground with basil, olive oil and Parmesan or peccorino cheese—whichever I have to hand. It takes longer to talk about than it takes to make,' she explained, reaching up to unhook a large copper saucepan from the rack above the table.

Garett would have done it for her, but admiring the graceful movements of her body as she stretched up meant he was a fraction too slow. Instead he offered to fill the pot with water, and put it on the range.

She was already tossing pinenuts in a frittata pan.

'Now I must fetch a big bunch of basil from Ermanno's greenhouse. That is what takes the time, but I can chop it while these are cooling.'

He stepped in and took the skillet from her, putting up a finger to silence any complaints. 'You could clearly do with a hand. I'll do this while you go out in the garden.'

'Keep those kernels on the move—you only want them toasted, not too dark. There's a knack to tossing them—you might be better off stirring them with this wooden spoon—'

'I'll be fine.' he said firmly. And he was. By the time Sienna dashed back into the kitchen with a fragrant bouquet of *Genovese dolce*, he was flipping the pinenuts like a professional.

'Garett! I am impressed!'

'That's nothing compared to the reaction I shall get when I recreate this for Kane and Molly.'

'They won't want to eat *povera* food like this.' Sienna giggled.

'Ah, you never know. This might be a dish that travels well. Without you throwing it at my head, that is.'

She stopped laughing. 'I wouldn't do that.'

You might if you knew the promise you made so painfully might all be for nothing, Garett thought, but he returned her smile.

She washed the basil and shook it dry in a cloth. A head of garlic hanging by the fireplace was raided for fat cloves, which she pounded in a basin with the pinenuts he tipped in from the pan. Grated cheese and the basil leaves were added at the last moment, to retain all their fragrance.

'The water is boiling. I'll put the pasta in for you.' Garett was halfway to the range before he had finished speaking.

Sienna dithered. He had been a fast learner with the skillet, but fresh pasta was so easily overcooked.

'Don't worry—if you could slice some extra Parmesan, I'll start the stracchi. In the time it takes them to cook we will have finished the sauce.'

'Co-operation, eh?' He chuckled, and Sienna felt again the lurch of desire that had tumbled her emotions before she had made her promise.

She went to fetch a new can of olive oil from the larder, expecting to be glad of any excuse to move away from him. Instead, she returned faster than she'd left. While he shaved paper-thin slices from a slab of Parmesan, Sienna tore the pasta into thin sheets. Slipping a few stracchi into the boiling water, she checked her watch. There was just time to thin the pesto with a stream of delicate gold-green oil and bring down a plate from the cupboard beside the range. Placing it on the table, she took cutlery out from a drawer and began looking around for a tray. With a sigh she realised her stepmother must have forgotten to bring the breakfast things down from her suite. Again.

'I'm afraid it looks as though you'll have to carry your own lunch through to the drawing room, Mr Lazlo.'

'We'll eat right here. Why make extra work and give the food a chance to go cold?' He said, straightening up and pushing both hands through his hair. The cut was so good that its midnight darkness fell straight back into place. 'It is hot in here, though—I never know how people survive without air-con.'

'The kitchen should cool down a bit when I've closed the range. If you could open all the windows a bit wider while I finish the pasta, that would make more of a through-draught.'

If the heat troubled him, he was hiding it well. As he passed close behind her to reach the windows, Sienna could not resist taking in an extra deep breath. Warmth was enlivening the discreet resinous tang of his aftershave. It was an intimate fragrance that made her think of woodland glades and dark, mysterious forests.

'Are you all right, Sienna?'

She looked up at him—and suddenly 'all right' hardly covered the feelings that flooded through her body. Garett in the flesh was even better than her fantasies. He was absolutely lovely—and in the not-too-distant future she would be sleeping with him. Right at this moment he was within touching distance. Surely if she made a move he would respond in kind? For long seconds Sienna could not speak. She was torn between getting the awful business over and done with and the dancing possibility that it might be somehow *different* with Garett…

Then bubbling water erupted over the side of the pasta pan, and she had to tear herself away.

'I'm fine, Garett—and luckily so is the stracchi!' She kept her laughter light, and hoped he had not picked up on her nervousness. After draining the pasta, she carried the pan to the table while he took a seat. Giving him all the stracchi, she picked up the bowl of freshly prepared pesto and offered that to him, too.

'Aren't you having any?' He cast a faintly disapproving look at her.

'Not at the moment—I had a proper breakfast,' she said virtuously as he spooned pesto over his lunch. Taking the dish when he had finished, she handed him the bowl of Parmesan shavings. 'Have as much as you like.'

He did. The surge of passion Sienna felt whenever she looked at him was almost outdone by her happiness at the sight of his healthy appetite. She loved it when people enjoyed her cooking. It was the one thing in her life about which she felt secure. From billionaires to farm workers— everyone needed to eat. Sienna had discovered a talent for feeding them—and a pleasure in seeing their pleasure, too.

With her eyes on her guest's plate, Sienna moved to take the basin of pesto from him. It was slick with oil, and her fingers slipped. Although she did not drop the dish, she knocked the spoon and sent a splash of pesto onto her hand. Without thinking, she raised her hand to her mouth and licked off the spilled sauce. She was so used to eating alone that it was the most natural thing in the world. She closed her eyes, revelling in every last drop of the unctuous liquor. Then a tiny noise reminded her that she had company. Her lids flew open—and she found herself gazing straight into Garett's eyes. He had put down his fork and was watching her.

His scrutiny was too intense. Sienna felt his attention trapping her like an embrace. Suddenly she was conscious of each and every breath sighing in and out of her body as desire laid siege to her respectability.

Garett swallowed, and realized his throat had gone dry. She had that effect on him. 'Aren't you going to offer me anything to drink?'

His words snapped her back into life and she emerged from her trance. There was nothing for it now but to look at him directly and ask what he would like. When she raised her head, she saw with a pang that he was still observing her, even as he ate.

'Coffee, if you have any.' Then he saw her expression and smiled. *'Please.'*

Garett watched her take the kettle to fill it at the sink.

He thought about the way her eyes had locked with his, only a moment before. Despite her obvious terror about what might be in store for her, for a second or two they had been full of smouldering promise. It was as though the universe had consisted of him and him alone.

Garett knew from past experience that he could have taken her then and there, as he had taken a hundred other women.

With a start, he rounded on himself savagely. What sort of thinking is that? The girl is clearly put upon, isolated and lonely. She's still in mourning, and missing her husband. I'm unaccustomed to that sort of frailty in women. I've merely mistaken it for attraction, that's all, his analytical mind told him.

But Garett Lazlo's body was purely primitive. It was accustomed to working on instinct, not analysis. As Sienna moved about the kitchen making coffee, her every movement aroused him. She was irresistible, but after seeing the fear in her eyes he had sworn not to taste her temptation. Now her body had become an instrument of torture for him. It was fascinating.

He was silent over coffee, struggling with his impulses. If he seduced her now he would break the spell she had cast over his body. The trouble was that would torment her—and break the promise he had made to himself. Nothing would persuade him to do either, he told himself.

But it was the look of terror in Sienna's eyes that haunted him more than any fanciful ideas about honour.

'Where would you like to start?' Sienna asked Garett later, as she led him out into the yard. The sooner she could demonstrate to the outside world—and to herself—that this was nothing more than a professional visit, the better. It didn't matter that no one was about: Sienna knew the locals watched the movements of every stranger in Piccia. Garett's arrival would have been noticed, if not his departure.

'I'll begin by working around the boundary,' he announced. 'Give me an idea of where it runs.'

'Ermanno will have finished in the dairy by now—I'll give him a call and he can escort you—'

'You don't need to do that. My everyday life is so noisy with people jostling for attention it will be a pleasure to explore such a beautiful place on my own. I can get much more done, and at a faster pace. Besides, I prefer working alone.'

'Oh, so do I!' Sienna said with real feeling. 'But it would be as well if Ermanno and his wife knew what you were doing. I wouldn't want them to think you were an intruder. And at this time of year you will need to watch out for vipers coming out to warm up in the sun.'

'Isn't it me that you consider to be the snake?' he murmured, then gave himself a virtual kick as he watched Sienna's eyes widen at the smoky meaning behind his words.

Although it was a dangerous situation, delight fizzed through Sienna's veins like Asti. Then she flinched. She desperately needed his expertise in checking over her estate, but it would be at the expense of her good name. If Imelda looked out and saw her talking alone to a man like Garett, her respectable disguise would be no protection any more. She would be married off to hideous cousin Claudio in a flash—before Garett could act.

Oh, *damn* respectability! Sienna suddenly thought to herself, with a violence that alarmed her. If only she could let Garett pull her bodily and mentally into his world. Relationships for a man like him must be free and fun, not handcuffed by other people's expectations. I'll bet Garett never insists meals are taken in silence in case his staff gossip, she thought bitterly.

After that one, distant night he might even bring me breakfast in bed, with flowers, and champagne…

'I hope you aren't trying to tempt me before time, Garett?' Sienna's heart gave a double thump. She had intended the words to be a crisp, businesslike warning, but something unexpected had happened. They'd come out sounding husky and provocative instead.

He raised his eyebrows, looking down at her with such sensual amusement in his dark eyes that she knew at once what was going through his mind. She blossomed despite herself as warmth ran through her veins like sunlight. It pushed back her shadows—for all of ten seconds.

'Would I do a thing like that?' He arched one dark eyebrow. 'Although…perhaps you *had* better call for your man Ermanno, Sienna.'

'Who? Oh, yes. Of course.'

I've made her blush, Garett realised with an unusual pang. Then she passed the tip of her tongue over her lips and he found himself holding his breath. He was so used to women coming on to him and flirting that he barely noticed them any more. So why did Sienna's tiny, involuntary action feel like such a triumph? Conflicting urges powered through his body. He wanted to protect her, but at the same time he felt as hot for her as any teenager. There was no way he could risk putting a comforting arm around her shoulders. The way he felt, it wouldn't stop there. Shifting uncomfortably, he looked away. This wasn't supposed to be happening. Business came first, and he had a lot to achieve here. That should be his first consideration, beyond keeping his physical responses under complete control. It was all part of not letting anyone get too close to the real Garett Lazlo.

Sienna was in trouble with her feelings as well. I must keep this on a purely business footing, she thought. Taking a step back, she called out for Ermanno. She sensed that

Garett was on the brink of making something happen. Something that would fulfil all her fantasies—and her fears.

Distraction came just in time. When Ermanno sprang into view, she was torn between relief and disappointment. As she gave him instructions to show their visitor around, Sienna's mind was in a whirl. Garett promised all sorts of things with his eyes. But her experiences with Aldo had taught her never to expect anything good from a man.

A name on a marriage certificate is enough, Imelda had told her. You don't need anything more.

But I did, Sienna yearned to herself. And I *do*...

This sudden independence of thought alarmed her. But in some exciting, illicit way it was fun.

'Ermanno will show you the extent of my land, and the things we do here.' She took off her apron and shook it, sending a cloud of flour into the air. Tying the strings around her narrow waist again gave her one good excuse not to look at Garett. 'I must go back inside and finish my baking.'

'Do you speak English, Ermanno?' she heard him say as the farm manager walked towards them across the yard. It made her smile.

'He knows enough to be able to give you a tour, Garett.'

But not enough to reveal anything about me, she thought, brushing the last streaks of flour from her apron.

'I'm sorry you won't be seeing things at their best. It's been a bad winter, and I haven't really been able to get back on top of things since Aldo died.' Her spirits sank with every hesitant word. Why on earth had she agreed to all this? The man Molly called the world's greatest trouble-shooter was bound to come up with winning ideas—but it was going be at such a heavy price.

Garett watched her head droop. It looked as though the ghost of her old husband would always be on hand, manning the barrier she kept raising. He smiled, put out a hand as though to cup her shoulder, but stopped before making contact. Withdrawing it, he murmured, 'I understand what you must be going through, Sienna. You will never be able to forget your husband, but with each passing day his memory will be encouraging you to carry on living your life in the way he would have liked.'

Her head went up at that, but when their eyes met he watched the words die on her lips. Instead she stayed silent, gazing at him with an expression he could not fathom.

It must be love. That's why I don't recognise it, he thought with cynical amusement. A long apprenticeship in the school of hard knocks had given him immunity.

'I tell you what, Sienna. Why don't you come around the grounds with us? Ermanno can act as chaperon.'

He expected her to back away rapidly at the idea, mindful of her reputation as always. Instead, she looked down to where she was idly drawing a line in the dust between them with the toe of her sandal.

Desperate that Ermanno should not see her disappointment, she shook her head. 'Thank you for your kind offer, Mr Lazlo, but I must get back to the kitchen. When my stepmother learns about you, I am sure you will gain a proper invitation into the house.'

'I'll look forward to that,' he assured her, trying to sound believable.

To Sienna's amazement, Imelda Basso was not remotely impressed by the idea of a foreigner entering her territory—even if he *was* a top-flight businessman. The second Sienna mentioned he was a friend of the Bradleys, Garett Lazlo received the social kiss of death. Imelda would not believe Kane and Molly had money. She considered that they lived too quietly, and that any acquaintance of theirs was likely to be telling equally tall tales about wealth and status. Imelda always needed to see money being spent, not just hear about it.

Sienna retreated to her room. Later, she watched from her window as her visitor strolled up through the overgrown terraces of olive trees at the end of his tour. Ermanno must have found something else to do, because Garett was sauntering towards the house alone. One hand in his pocket, he looked around him with the air of a man who could make himself at home anywhere. But not here, Sienna thought, springing out of her trance. She ran downstairs, desperate to get to him before he could reach the heavy iron doorknocker.

'You certainly have a beautiful place here.' He laughed. The light breeze had tousled his hair and the warm sun had undone several of his buttons. 'When I was up on that far ridge I could see sunlight glittering on the sea, right in the distance.'

'I know. It is one of the compensations of living here.'

He put his head on one side, frowning.

'That's a strange thing to say.'

Sienna clasped her hands. They were damp. She felt nervous, having revealed her true feelings. 'Er…that is…it is one of the *delights* of living here. I'm sorry—my English sometimes lets me down…'

He did not look convinced.

'It would be a pity to lose it.' He was looking at her acutely. 'I'll be perfectly honest with you, Sienna. I need to get working right away. In fact, it would be better if I came in now and made a start. You can sort me out space for a site office—'

'No!'

He was already heading for the kitchen door, but Sienna moved to block him. 'I mean…my stepmother has forbidden it.'

He nipped at his lower lip.

'The time for listening to her has gone, *signora*. You are going to have to start putting yourself first—and fast.'

There was a strange echo of Molly's words in what Garett was telling her now. Sienna might ignore her own needs, but within the past day two different people—Garett and the old *nonna* at the market—had told her to follow her instincts. And that was without Molly and Kane's constant nagging about Imelda's treatment of her.

Sienna hesitated—but only for a second.

'Very well—but I can't possibly let you into the house now that my stepmother has refused.'

'Excuse me—whose house is this?'

'Mine.' Sienna missed the irony in his tone. She was distracted, casting around the outbuildings and trying to decide where they might talk in private, yet without causing a scandal. 'You can work in the lemon shelter. It is an open-fronted shed where the potted orchard used to be kept during the winter—'

His mind was too busy for explanations. He was already walking away.

'I'm off to set up the headquarters of the Entroterra project

in a corner of Kane and Molly's villa. The moment you can
convince yourself you can get away, come over and see me.'

And with that he was gone.

Garett's first conclusions about Sienna's estate were
gloomy. Her future seemed bleak. Leaving his hire-car
outside her kitchen, he decided to walk back to the
Bradleys' villa. It would give him plenty of time to think.

Cruising around the Mediterranean had seemed an ideal
way to avoid the pressures and stress of New York City life.
He had thought he could escape by throwing money at his
problems, paying in cash to remain anonymous and
evading all calls from his office. He had accepted the
Bradleys' invitation to stay in the hope of finding an answer
to the dissatisfaction that tormented him. Instead he found
himself adrift on a whole new raft of puzzles.

As an intensely private person, he had thought the
novelty of company might help. He was accustomed to
having staff on hand every hour of the day and night, but
that was not quite the same as having a friendship. Garett
caught himself shying away from the word 'relationship'.
It conjured up all sorts of bad memories. His only mean-
ingful one to date had ended when he was six years old. That
was when he had watched his father kill his mother. From
that moment on Garett had vowed never to put any woman
in such a vulnerable position. That was why he did not stay
too long in one place. Lingering made people—especially
women—start thinking about commitment. Garett made a
point of committing only to work. It proved a harsh
mistress, but his loyalty had paid off a billion times over.

He was concentrating on that achievement when a

sound stirred his unquiet conscience. He turned to locate the source and saw, twenty yards away, Ermanno approaching the open door of a small house adjoining the yard. A woman stood there, a flour-streaked apron covering her sensible black skirt and blouse. She had a mixing bowl in her hand, and as Garett watched she held the spoon out to Ermanno to taste. Existing on a diet of split-second timing and vending machine coffee, Garett was touched. The scene reminded him of the false intimacy he had shared with Sienna over her pasta-making. What *was* it about home cooking? It always looked such fun. Perhaps women felt a deep-seated urge to create something, and as a man he was genetically programmed to appreciate it. Or were they naturally more generous than men, and liked to share?

He wanted to go on watching Ermanno and his wife, but found he had to look away. The moment was too intimate. Garett regularly dined with princes, and probably earned more in one minute than a farm worker saw in a year, but in those sixty seconds Garett sensed that Ermanno possessed something that he had never owned—peace of mind.

CHAPTER EIGHT

SIENNA presented herself at the Bradleys' front door within the hour. A maid showed her into a small room leading off the main lobby. Sienna had been in there many times before, but it was unrecognisable now. Every horizontal surface was covered with spreadsheets, and computer hardware and software. Garett sat in the middle of this organised chaos. Phone clamped to his ear, he was rocking back in his chair as he made some complicated arrangements for sub-contracting labour.

'What have you done to Molly's craft room?' Sienna gasped, the moment he finished his call.

'She won't mind. Kane's taken her off on a shopping trip to Portofino.'

'That is a long way to go on a whim, at this time of day,' Sienna said suspiciously.

'Oh? And I thought you Europeans enjoyed stretching each day to the max,' he teased. 'I've already hired back all the builders who worked on this house. The proof of their good work is all around me. But now I need you and your beautiful native tongue to put some more complicated concepts to the firms on this list—' He pulled a sheet of paper out of the computer's printer tray and flourished it at her.

'Oh—no—I couldn't possibly—I haven't come here to work!' Sienna held up her hands and started backing away. 'What will people say? The whole village will be alight with gossip—'

Broken sentences tumbled over one another as she gabbled her way towards the door. She was as anxious to escape as her words, but Garett put a stop to it all. He beat her to the exit in half a dozen long strides. Putting out his hand to the doorframe, he barred her way.

'Oh, no, you don't! If you're genuine about wanting to save Aldo's villa, then you are going to have to give me a hand. I achieve miracles every day of my working life. I will do it for you, too. But to pull off a near-impossible project like this one I will need your help.'

It was that honey voice of his—the one that always threatened to turn her self-control into a memory. Sienna gulped. He was within centimetres of her, so close that she could feel the warmth radiating from him.

'I can do this, but not without your help.'

His voice breathed through her confusion. Without knowing why, she raised her hands in an almost childlike gesture. She was about to apologise, but he gave her no time. Impulse overtook him at that moment, and he kissed her.

It was supposed to be a gesture of reassurance. Simple, unthreatening proof that he would go only so far, but no further. It did not turn out like that.

The moment his lips touched hers, he felt all the tension leave her body. She melted like marshmallow in chocolate fondue. The effect transformed him in a heartbeat. Her perfume felt like balm. She was all fresh air and flowers, mingled with simple human warmth. It aroused such a yearning in him that his kiss went on, and on. He kissed her until her mouth opened—not in fear or complaint, but in invitation. Garett had heard that the mind went blank while kissing. It had never yet happened to him. He prided himself on keeping his wits about him at all times. That was what made him such a success. So this kiss was something he fully intended to enjoy to the full. Gradually, he allowed the tip of his tongue to test her, to tease her, flickering over the plump cushions of her lips but venturing no further.

Let other men have their virgins—once a woman discovers sex there is no holding her, he thought, rejoicing in the supple warmth of her body. She swayed, and leaned against him heavily. Is it just for support, or to test me? he wondered. Then all of a sudden his mind dissolved. Her body was pressing against him. In that moment, all his other experiences counted for nothing. This was the only one that mattered. Yet he wanted gratification, nothing more. That was what he kept telling himself. Sienna di Imperia could mean nothing to him. Although she had such passivity and inner beauty… He had never encountered things like this in any other woman. He had to have her—here, now—

Sienna began to want him. The air escaped from her lungs in a little gasp of pleasure. Closing her eyes, she touched her lips to his again. It was a hesitant gesture that he was only too quick to capitalise upon. Cupping her head with his hands, he kissed her once more, with a passion that burned like fire. The suddenness was too much. It lashed Sienna out of her trance and she leapt back as though burned.

No—this was all wrong. She wanted him, but she

did not want the emotionless sex of this bargain. There had been too much of that in her recent past. That was why she had to put a distance between her and Garett. She was too physically frail to resist him. She was used to losing her dignity beneath the crushing weight of male authority—but that was nothing like this. What happened when Garett kissed her was far more frightening than that. In those first few seconds of unbridled passion she had almost lost her mind.

She braced her hands against his shoulders and shook her head.

'No. I cannot. It is too soon—'

Garett was breathing fast. Restraint was not in his sexual nature. Waiting—plans—challenges—they could all go to hell. He had sampled her kisses, and now he wanted more. That was the only thing that mattered.

'Would you do this to save Aldo's inheritance?' His breath whispered past her cheek.

Sienna's fingers tightened on his arms. She closed her eyes. If only it was as easy to shut out her problems by retreating behind the small, well-loved front door she had left behind so regretfully, so long ago.

'For the villa?' She could not confess, and looked away. 'If I thought I could go back to my own little house in the village and never be bothered with anyone or anything ever again then, yes—yes, I would sell my very soul…'

Her voice had been steady, but her legs were shaking as she pulled herself out of his grasp. Walking out of the room, she slammed the door behind her with a report that thundered through the whole house.

* * *

Sienna walked away from the Bradleys' villa with her head held high. It was only when she was out of sight of the house that her eyes began to fill. She blundered off the gritty track and into the hazel grove that bordered her route home. Standing in a clearing, she cried furious tears of disappointment and frustration.

In an instant she had gone from ecstasy to terror. Once again Garett had ignited sparks within her body—and then stifled the curling, smoky tendrils of her passion by moving in on her straight away. He was going to break his side of the bargain. She knew it, and there was nothing she could do about it. His body was too much of a temptation. But if she gave in, he would have no incentive to work on her house. And if she refused him, there was nothing to stop him walking away. Both options had the power to drive her insane. She desperately wanted to run—to escape. But there *was* no escape. All she wanted was to retreat to the little cottage where she had grown up. But Imelda would never stoop to moving there, and with no hope of saving the building anyway without Garett's help she was cursed. She would have to stay here, on this land and in Aldo's villa, which was crammed with so many bad memories.

She was trapped. Her father must have found something in Imelda to love, so Sienna knew it was her duty to care for the woman. It didn't matter about her own feelings. She had to keep in mind what her father would have wanted. Caring for Imelda meant staying at Entroterra—and that needed money. Imelda's plan was to move old Claudio into the property with them, but it was a price Sienna did not want to pay. Her refusal had kept the atmosphere simmering at home since Aldo's funeral. It boiled over into open warfare whenever Imelda brought the subject up.

Now Garett was offering her an escape from that. All she had to do was sit tight and endure for just a short while longer. Then her problems would be over—but only as long as he kept his side of the bargain. Garett had explained he would be providing finance to restore her properties and land. Then, once everything was under way, it would all be mortgaged in Sienna's sole name. That meant he must make a start right now, pouring his own money directly into the Entroterra estate. He would be in full control of all the finances at all times, and Imelda would be unable to bully her way into spending any of it.

Sienna tried to console herself with the idea that sacrificing her body would save Aldo's house and the good name of his ancient family. And giving Garett an excuse to stay in the area would be sure to delight her friends Molly and Kane too. Also, wonder of wonders, living in a clean, warm, light house might even keep Imelda quiet— at least for a while.

But it meant that Sienna would have to give her body to a man who treated sex like a hobby. Otherwise, how could he think of using it as a bargaining tool?

Sienna had never forgiven herself for agreeing to marry Aldo. She had made the best of it then, because it had safeguarded all her father's property. Now she would have to desert her principles a second time. Desperate circumstances had pushed her at Aldo. This time she was faced with selling herself to Garett. But was that really any worse than marrying Claudio, simply in the hope that

Aldo's rich cousin could silence Imelda's continual demands for cash?

Garett was everything Sienna could ever want in a man—he was gorgeous, he was clever, he even admired her knitting. Best of all, he liked her cooking. Sienna knew there would never be any other man for her.

But now her dream was turning into a nightmare. In reality, he was proving to be no different from Aldo. He wanted the one thing Sienna was afraid to give him.

But something had to be done to safeguard Aldo's property and the other little home she loved. And surely Garett Lazlo was the man to do it? But he had blown into her life so suddenly. He could vanish with equal ease. He was brisk and efficient, certainly, but that was now—when he still had her in his sights. Who was to say he really had the determination and patience to do his best for places that had existed for hundreds of years?

He was the most incredible man she had ever met. But Sienna knew she could not let that blind her to his dangers. She only had one thing in her favour. He really did want her. She had seen it in his eyes and felt it under the keen pressure of his fingertips. There was no faking the physical reaction she ignited in him, and Sienna's mind flickered with sudden hope.

She would have to keep a tighter curb on her own body. If she was careful, she might turn the one thing he wanted more than anything else into a weapon. She would hold it against him—but nothing more—until his work on the estate was completed. Only when she was satisfied would he get his own satisfaction.

* * *

Garett made no move to follow Sienna when she left. To do so would be counter-productive—and anyway, he knew he did not need to. She would be back. Sooner or later.

Head down, he worked on without a break until it was time to go up and change for dinner. His suite was as welcoming as ever, but he was not in a mood to appreciate it. The computer-controlled shower in his marble and silver wet room was the last word in luxury. One touch provided a deliciously warm tropical downpour. But that was not what Garett needed right now. Stripping off his clothes, he adjusted the thermostat and dived in. Freezing needles of ice assaulted his hard, toned muscles.

He tried to organise his thoughts. All he could see was Sienna's face. People tended to smile at him only when they wanted something. Garett had taught himself not to trust any of them. But Sienna was an unknown quantity.

He worked hard, he worked alone, and he worked incessantly. Recent events had shocked him into realising that there must be another way. The flashpoint had come when he'd erupted at a street kid who'd happened to follow him for a couple of blocks, hoping for quarters. Garett had found himself looming over the terrified boy like a playground bully, and hating himself for doing it. Hell— not so long ago, *he* had been that little guy! The thought that success was turning him into one of the loveless, paranoid monsters who had wrecked his own childhood had horrified Garett. That last day in Manhattan had been a wake-up call for his conscience. He had escaped, turned his back on everything he knew.

This unexpected stay with the Bradleys was good for him. They were decent people, who usually kept him in touch with reality. But he couldn't help thinking that they had confronted him with a dream. Sienna was everything he could ever want in a woman—beautiful, and infinitely charming. Not that it meant much, in the final reckoning. Garett knew women, and, however shy and retiring Sienna di Imperia might appear at the moment, in the end she would turn out to be just like all the rest. Once she fell fully for his charms those long, lovely lashes would start to flutter like a flurry of euros. Women wanted pleasure and they wanted money. Garett knew he was the man to supply both in an endless supply—until he got bored.

He shook himself, momentarily startled. He was supposed to be on holiday. Revelling in thoughts of pleasure was one thing. Acting on them was quite another. And it was out of the question for now. He had isolated himself from his business to give himself a holiday from all things stressful—including women. Working for the Entroterra estate was nothing special—it was simply a matter of keeping his hand in. He was certain that doing nothing but laze about on his new yacht or here in the Bradleys' villa would have killed him off within hours. Keeping his mind active with Sienna's project would be much more pleasurable. His body was being kept nicely alert by the power of his mind, and he could delight in playing Sienna like a beautiful silver salmon, bending her to his will without the slightest danger to his heart…

Deep down in her own heart, Sienna knew Garett could take her body as easily as he overwhelmed her mind. All it would take was one touch, one glance, and she would be lost. He had never needed to put his bargain into words.

For her, it was a natural progression. She had been attracted to him from the moment he strode into Portofino market. In those first few moments catching the eye of a man like him had seemed an impossible dream. And then he had talked to her—Sienna! The sound of his voice had stolen her heart and the firm mastery of his touch had secured it for ever. Her emotions were all his—but unfortunately her mind was still her own. It kept reminding her that this was a man who saw her body as a prize. Someone who could do that must be capable of anything.

Sienna was in an impossible position. It was either submit to Garett or succumb to Aldo's cousin Claudio—a straight choice between a smooth deceiver and a devious runt.

And that, as she already knew, was no choice at all.

Sienna was desperate—desperate enough to swallow her pride. Garett was right, of course. She needed to make her property work for itself if she was to catch her dream of moving back to the little village house of her childhood. The glimmer of independence was beginning to tempt her, but Imelda's eyes were glittering brighter with thoughts of tying rich old Claudio to their bank account. That was the easiest way, her stepmother argued. It did not involve foreigners, work or expense.

Sienna stood her ground. At least Garett's solution was honestly dishonest. It did not involve selling herself publicly, through a golden wedding ring.

Next day, she put on the black linen jacket and gored skirt she had bought for Aldo's funeral. Wrapping her velvet stilettos in a plastic bag, she walked over to the Bradleys' house. While still out of sight, in the hazel grove, she changed into the impractically beautiful sandals. If she was going to work for a man like Garett, she was going to look the part. Hiding her sensible-but-dull loafers among the coppiced hazel stumps, she smoothed down her skirt and neatened her collar, then made her way gingerly up the final slope.

As this was a formal visit, she went straight to the high-gloss black front door. A uniformed maid opened it, and told her that the master and mistress were out for the day. Sienna had spent her walk rehearsing how she would avoid breaking down and telling Molly about Garett's designs on her honour. Now she did not know what to do. All her good intentions evaporated and she dithered on the doorstep.

'Signora di Imperia!'

Before Sienna could move, or hide, or do anything at all, Garett's impressive figure swaggered down the wide marble staircase. He was turning back the cuffs of his white shirt, adding to the casual air about him. His open collar displayed a hint of body hair, and his smile widened as he saw her notice it.

'You nearly missed me,' he said, dismissing the maid with a nod. 'I've got everything well underway with regard to your estate, so I thought I'd factor in a little R and R. Kane says I can borrow his plane to slide over to Nice for a few hours. What do you reckon? You certainly look dressed for a day on the town.'

Sienna thought of the irresistible Mediterranean, lined with jostling sightseers and petulant rich people.

'I think you will enjoy yourself, Garett. I'm sorry to have disturbed you.' She was already turning away, but he reached out and placed a hand on her shoulder.

'But you haven't. Why don't you come with me?'

She could not argue with the hold he had over her, but she could make a stand.

'No, thank you—I came here to work this morning, Mr Lazlo.'

'It's good to hear that. Not a problem. We can do it in Nice, out of everybody's earshot.' He tipped his head in the direction of the retreating maid. As he spoke, his fingers glided down the length of Sienna's arm and grasped her hand. He was already out of the door, but she refused to be dragged along in his wake. Sensing that this was a serious moment, he stopped and looked down at her expectantly.

Sienna hoped he could not hear her knees trembling. 'I said that I came here to work, and I meant it, Mr Lazlo.'

'I didn't doubt you for a moment, *signora*.' He smiled lazily.

Sienna tried her hardest to maintain the formal air between them, even though she could sense he was mocking her. 'I'm glad you feel that way, Mr Lazlo, because I have a proposition to put to you—a decent one, before you revive any ideas about what happened yesterday. I desperately need help with my house, but I hardly slept last night for thinking about—well, for trying to reconcile my longing to reclaim my past with the fact that I must live in the present. I've decided that I cannot sacrifice my body to you. I would rather you sold my father's properties in the village to fund work on the Entroterra estate. Then I won't owe you anything—money, or…any other sort of obligation,' she finished with difficulty.

He regarded her with narrowed eyes. Gradually, his hold on her hand loosened.

'So…you won't be included in the deal?'

'No.'

He dropped her hand altogether.

'But you've told me how much that house means to you, Sienna.

'It means the world to me.' She held his gaze.

He dug his hands deep into his pockets and shrugged. 'Fine. I'll make arrangements for an agent to value your father's properties, and we can see how far that will get us with work on the villa.'

Sienna looked at him quizzically. 'You don't mind?'

'Why should I? If you've thought this through and come to a decision without any prompting from me, then I respect that. That's all there is to it. We'll forget all about the other…arrangement.' He looked away from her across the courtyard, as though the sparrows squabbling on the cobbles meant more to him than she did.

This was not the reaction Sienna had expected. She had needed all her courage to come out with this new idea, and had been expecting him to refuse. Instead, he was treating the whole thing as just another meeting in his busy schedule.

'Is that it?' she said eventually, when the suspense of his silence became too much for her.

'What do you mean? You surely weren't expecting me to beg? I'm not that sort of man. You've made your decision, and that's all there is to it. You've made a stand— possibly for the first time in your life—and I respect that,' he said, nonchalantly.

His nonchalance felt worse to Sienna than his fury would have done. If she had ever tried refusing sex in the past, it had always increased Aldo's annoyance rather than defusing it.

'Thank you,' Sienna said brightly, but her heart was dark. She was supposed to feel relieved. Yet she felt empty, let down, and—to her disbelief—disappointed.

Garett nodded, wondering why he felt neither thankful nor released.

He decided against driving his hire car to the airfield where Kane kept his plane. Instead, he called into the Bradleys' garage block.

'If we're going to be borrowing the plane, we might as well borrow a Mercedes too,' he said, holding open the rear door of a silver blue saloon for Sienna to step in.

She took a while to come to terms with such luxury. Aldo had owned a large top-of-the-range Fiat but it had been as old as Ermanno's donkey. This beautiful car was sleek, new, and softly upholstered. She spread her hands over the seats, marvelling at how anyone could keep cream upholstery so clean.

'All it takes is enough money to keep a fleet of staff.' Garett read her thoughts as he settled himself in the seat beside her. 'Now, just in case your properties don't provide enough funds to complete the Entroterra project, I wonder if you have any contingency plans to save yourself from my clutches?' he mused.

'Shh!' Sienna's eyes darted guiltily toward the back of the driver's head.

'Kane's staff are as discreet as they are hardworking.' Garett smiled, but all the same he raised the glass partition separating them from the chauffeur. Sitting back, he fastened his seat belt and gestured for her to do the same.

Sienna squirmed. She was having difficulty in getting comfortable. Unused to the sleek lines of her closely fitted skirt, she needed freedom to move. Unaware that one of his passengers was not yet secure, the chauffeur pulled away from the parking bay. The Mercedes surged forward with the smooth expense of power. Without the security of her seat belt Sienna was thrown across the car.

Garett acted purely on instinct. As she was jolted against him he grabbed her, and held her tight.

'And I thought you'd reconsidered!' He chuckled.

Sienna's face was pressed against the fine material of his white shirt. She could feel his heart beating, slow and rhythmically, against the broad expanse of his chest. It should have been reassuring. Instead it accelerated her own pulse to fever-pitch. Knowing that one more second would destroy all her good intentions, Sienna pushed herself upright. Her hair swung across her face, hiding her confusion as she made a great show of fastening her seat belt.

'I'm sorry about that. It should never have happened,' she said stiffly. The heat from his body had transferred to her, and the thin blouse she was wearing beneath her formal jacket suddenly felt painfully restricting. The nearness of him always had such an effect on her. Feeling his body so close to hers whipped her hormones into a frenzy of expectation. She could feel the delicate points of her nipples teasing against the lace of her bra, and hoped their arousal was not visible through her clothes.

'Accidents can happen,' he said mildly.

If he was showing any interest in her body, Sienna was too embarrassed to notice. She pressed herself into the corner of the car, unwilling to give him any inkling of the physical attraction his body had for hers.

'Not to me they don't. Not any more,' Sienna decided aloud.

'Then why don't you outline your back-up scheme for the Entroterra estate's salvation?'

Sienna looked down at her hands. Her fingers were trembling. She clasped them, hoping that was something else he would not notice.

'Well…as you seem to like it in this area, *signor*, you could always help me and do yourself a favour at the same time—without involving…you know…' She hesitated.

He gave a knowing half-smile, and nodded for her to continue.

'I haven't quite worked out the details, but I thought if you bought into the Entroterra estate, you could have all the benefits of living here while I gain from your expertise at no cost to myself,' she said simply.

'Well, you're coming along the path to independence in leaps and bounds, aren't you?' He smiled, but then shook his head with regret. 'Thanks, but no thanks, *signora*. I've got all the houses I need, I'm afraid. The gypsy in my soul means I'd rather stay with Molly and Kane for a while, or holiday on my yacht. I don't need to buy in to property here.' The expression in his eyes spoke of far more than mere bricks and mortar.

Sienna looked out across the sun-dried countryside speeding past the car windows. This was her land. It was the place where she had run and played as a child. The only thing worse than forsaking it for a cramped city flat would be to marry Cousin Claudio and for him to start lording it here. She swallowed hard, forcing down the bitter taste of compromise.

'I can't possibly offer you anything more.' She raised

her hand, ready to clap her palm to the car seat between them and emphasise the point.

'And that is your final word?'

'Yes,' she said with emphasis, and lowered her hand. A new confidence surged through her veins. It might be that straight talking would work better with Garett than dramatic gestures.

Her confidence was misplaced. When he finally nodded, a strange look flickered across his face. Sienna was too busy congratulating herself to notice.

In your own quiet way you're becoming quite a force to be reckoned with, Signora di Imperia, he thought to himself. So let's see how you respond to being given a little bit more licence to live…

CHAPTER NINE

SIENNA stood in the sunshine, trying to keep her mind on the task in hand. Raising her sunglasses, she used them to push the thick glossy mane of hair back from her face. Two hours had passed since she had got the better of Garett Lazlo.

She smiled, remembering his watchful silence for the rest of their journey. The moment they'd touched down in Nice he had disappeared, leaving her with a gleaming and expensive new hire-car. He wanted to go his own way for a while, he had told her. She should see this as a taste of the new freedom his temporary investment in the Entroterra estate gave her, he'd said. It would also be a perfect opportunity for her to enjoy the sights and sounds of Nice.

It was only after he'd walked off and left her alone that Sienna had realised he was giving her a chance to stand on her own two feet for once. Imelda and Aldo had always driven and manipulated her. Garett was not like that. Instead, he played up the advantages that his methods could bring, and never mentioned the twin pillars of duty and obedience.

Go to the market and buy yourself some flowers, he had said. They will raise your spirits. Live as though you have ten thousand a year more to spend than you actually do. Act the part, and people will respect you as though your fantasy is real.

So now she stood in the florist's, checking off her purchases as they were packed into the car Garett had picked up at the airport. This was the sort of 'work' she liked, and she took a lot of pleasure from the fresh fragrance and greenery. Bewitched by the scent of the potted gardenias lining the florist's shop, Sienna asked on impulse for one to be included in her order. She had never done such a reckless thing before, but tried to convince herself it could be written off as a proper business expense. The flower would sit in the hall and overpower the faint smell of mushrooms that always hung about the old place.

With a sudden sense of wonder Sienna realised that only a short time ago she would never have dreamed of making such a purchase. The idea that Garett's motivation was already bringing her some pleasure washed over her like a warm sea. Then a hand slipped under her elbow, and she found herself awash with guilt instead.

It was Garett. He gave a silent whistle.

'You've really taken my suggestion to heart, haven't you?'

'Mr Lazlo—Garett—I hope I haven't been too extravagant—'

'I told you to spend what you like.' He smiled. 'Leave me to worry about the cost. Believe me, that's not a problem.' He looked around the shop with a confidence that announced he could have bought the whole place a dozen times over.

'And—talking about extravagance—I've booked us into a restaurant for lunch. You'd better finish here so we can set off.'

Sienna checked her watch. 'It's far too early. Did you come out without breakfast again?' She levelled a look at him, but he shook his head.

'After the way you reacted the last time? No. I want to pick up a few things on the way, that's all, so by the time we eventually get there our table should be waiting.'

Sienna was only too happy to agree. The shops in Nice were every bit as stylish and imposing as those in Portofino. Alone, she would never have had the nerve to do anything but window-shop in such a grand setting. With Garett, she could walk straight into places she would never have dreamed of entering. As they approached the first designer outlet, she tried to look as though she shopped like this every day. In reality, she was secretly sizing up all the crystal-encrusted cocktail dresses and svelte evening gowns with the expertise of a commercial spy.

Her excitement soon turned to alarm when she was whisked away into a fitting room and poured into a selection of outfits. Each one was more beautiful than the last. Sienna's task, her pencil-thin personal shopper told her, was to choose which ones she liked best.

'I can't see any price tags,' Sienna managed uncomfortably as she was paraded out for Garett's inspection wearing a Chanel suit in silk, with matching bag. He was leaning against a marble pillar, chatting with the impressively fashionable manageress.

'Oh, don't worry about that. Just make sure you choose something that will impress the agents and bank managers you are going to be meeting this week. And me,' he added, with rather more of a smile than Sienna liked. 'If you want to persuade me you've got the spirit to fend for yourself

130 ONE NIGHT IN HIS BED

once I've gone home to Manhattan, you can start by looking the part.'

The manageress gazed at him indulgently.

The staff were all so anxious to please that Sienna could not disappoint them. She smiled her practised smile—but she was uneasy. Standing in front of the full-length mirror while dressmakers flitted around her, Sienna interrogated her reflection. How could she let this perfect stranger buy her clothes and order her about?

The reason for that was only too obvious. Sienna needed clothes. The neatly folded pile of garments lying on the changing room vanity unit were the only new things she had bought in years. They had been purchased in a moment of dire necessity, for Aldo's funeral. Her late husband had hated spending money. He had considered that indestructible man-made fibres were the greatest discovery in the history of mankind. In order to keep Imelda dressed like the mother-in-law of a millionaire, Sienna had been forced to beg for a clothing allowance. The old man had been so reluctant that Sienna had never risked asking for anything for herself. Instead, she had repaired and restyled her existing clothes. The only time she got anything different to wear was when Imelda tired of a particular outfit. Then it would be passed down to her. Sienna would use panels of fabric removed from the width to lengthen Imelda's cast-offs, which led to some interesting results.

Now, today, the world's most desirable billionaire had flown her to Nice. He was driving her around in an electric blue cabriolet and buying her dresses from top designers. It wasn't right.

But it *was* nice.

She looked at all the window-shoppers jostling along on the pavements outside the shop. Any one of them would swap places with her in an instant. She had no right to be ungrateful. If money was what Garett understood, and he didn't want to buy into her property, then there was only one thing to do if she wanted to keep her integrity. She would have to sell something and pay him back. She could not allow herself to be in debt to him in any way.

While he settled up, Sienna tried to find out how much her new clothes had cost. Nobody in the shop would discuss money with her. She was left to guess. The idea of selling off something useless to settle her account with Garett began to appeal to her more and more. There was one particularly hideous oil painting leering down over a chimneybreast in the great hall back at home. It was the only thing that Sienna and her stepmother agreed about. Its dark depiction of contorted young men in various states of undress was, in Imelda's words, 'not quite nice'.

Perhaps Garett would take it away in settlement?

When she mentioned it, he was delighted that she was starting to think for herself, and knew instantly which picture she meant. He had spotted it on the first day, when he'd roamed around the ground floor of the villa on his own.

The moment they got home from Nice, he swung into action and rang someone to arrange for the picture to be checked out. The news was good—and from then on Garett felt completely reassured when he paid out on architects and builders. Without going into details before the picture was officially authenticated, he hinted to Sienna that Imelda would be better off not knowing anything about the investigations, and with a smile assured her that there would be enough security in the picture to satisfy him.

This turn of events finally convinced Garett that working on the Entroterra project was a good idea. He arranged for Sienna to visit banks and financial institutions on the strength of it. Insurance cover and bridging loans were put in place so that one day she would be able to pay back the money he was pouring into the refurbishments around her home and grounds.

Sleep had been difficult enough for Sienna when Garett was an untouchable fantasy. Now she was slipping further and further into his debt it was almost impossible. She not only worried about her own finances now, she grew increasingly suspicious about his apparently inexhaustible wealth. Several times during the dinner party at Kane and Molly's house the Bradleys had tried to get Garett to open up about the size of his fortune. Sienna had been quietly embarrassed at the time. Now she wished she had spoken up and encouraged him to explain his circumstances—although she hated herself for being so wrapped up in the subject of money.

Experience told her that Imelda was right, and that rich men offered security, but something deep within Sienna wanted to rebel. There must be more to life than lunging desperately from one financial lifebelt to another. Love…that is the thing I crave, she thought sadly. Piccia was full of families held together by bonds much stronger than paper and coins. They were poor, but honest and happy at the same time. Allegedly Garett Lazlo had everything they lacked, yet he always seemed so edgy and unsatisfied. Sienna was beginning to wonder if his conscience was troubling him. She decided to do some investigating.

The village co-operative was always glad of extra help, so one day, when her house was full of workmen and her garden full of machinery, Sienna offered to put in an extra day's work on the market stall. It would keep her out of everyone's way at home, and give her the perfect excuse to visit Portofino.

The minute her shift on the stall was over, she walked down to the harbour. The whole place was busy with summer, and everything smelled of new paint and money. Brightly coloured flags moved lazily in a light breeze, like pennons at a medieval tournament, and loving teams of polishers and engineers tended each luxury yacht as it waited on the gently breathing water. It was a whole new world—but Sienna did not have time for sightseeing. She was looking for one vessel in particular.

The Bradleys had been unable to get much information out of Garett about his new purchase, but Sienna was determined. She had started to see his silence about the yacht as slightly odd. From what Kane and Molly had told her about its size, and the number of crew, Sienna foresaw no problem in tracking it down. All she would need to do was ask around. Something that size would be noticeable, even in Portofino. Especially when a man like Garett Lazlo owned it, Sienna thought. It was rumoured that the crews employed by some rich people were only too happy to let visitors drool over the yachts at close quarters—for a price. Taking the last of her ready cash, she went off to find out.

She had expected it to be easy. Instead, nothing could have been more difficult. Nobody had heard of Garett Lazlo. She even screwed up her courage and spoke to some of the aristocratic blonde teenagers who draped themselves about the sundecks like trophies. They were hired by the season to provide cordon bleu cooking for image-conscious billionaires. That was exactly the type of thing Garett would invest in, Sienna thought—but, no. Despite cooing over her description, none of the girls knew anything about him.

Sienna returned to the market, deep in thought. The only thing that stopped her racing home to confront him immediately was her friendship with the Bradleys. If Molly and Kane liked him enough to let him stay in their luxury villa, then Garett couldn't possibly be the liar he seemed to be. Could he? She puzzled over the differences between the fantasy that was Garett Lazlo and his reality for the rest of the day.

'You're quiet, Sienna?' The co-operative's secretary probed as she drove them both back home from Portofino that afternoon.

'I'm always quiet, Anna Maria.' Sienna tried a smile.

'Yes, but this is a different sort of silence.' Her friend laughed, then stopped. 'Look over there—what's that plume of smoke?'

Sienna sat bolt upright in the passenger seat, straining forward to see through the branches of some roadside poplars.

'It's a fire—a fire at my place!'

Instantly Sienna forgot all her ideas about cornering Garett over his fictional boat. Anna Maria slammed her foot down on the accelerator. As the co-operative's tiny van reached Entroterra land, dancing flakes of ash added to the smell and crackle of burning that filled the air. Sienna's senses were overwhelmed, leaving no room for anything but panic.

'Wait—look—it's only a builder's bonfire.' Anna Maria

sighed with relief. Then suddenly her voice took on a smoky quality. 'And look who's in charge!'

'That's Garett.' Sienna felt herself blushing. He was stripped to the waist, muscles rippling, as he directed workman around the forecourt and buildings. Wreathed in smoke from the fire, it was some time before he looked around to see who was driving up.

'No wonder you've been quiet. A guy like that must give you a whole lot to think about!' Anna Maria was raking Garett's half-naked body with looks of unmistakable longing. He returned her gaze with a casual smile as he opened the van door to let Sienna out.

'Right…well, if there's no emergency here I'll be off, and leave you two to get on with…whatever it is you're going to be getting on with!' Anna Maria winked at Sienna, who was too furious to notice. She stood beside Garett, rigid with anger, until the co-operative's van careered off down the drive. Then she rounded on him.

'There is a great plume of smoke rising up from here! I was frightened to death! I expected to see this whole place burned to the ground. What the *hell* do you think you're doing?'

'I thought you wanted me to help save your future?'

'Yes, but at what cost?'

He treated her to a lopsided grin, and then looked away, across the scene of builders toiling away at every part of the building.

'Keep talking like that, Sienna, and I might start to think you're ready to manage without me.'

With his attention elsewhere, Sienna let her eyes be drawn to the sparkles of sweat beading his smooth, clear skin. As she watched, a trickle ran down over the taut muscles and disappeared into the dense mass of dark hair covering his pectorals. Without acknowledging her gaze, he turned aside and strolled over to a mechanical digger parked on the cobblestones. Pulling a cotton shirt from its cab, he dragged it on over his head. Unrolling the sleeves, he threw a few seemingly unimportant words over his shoulder.

'Is that better?' It was obvious he had caught her watching him.

Sienna flushed a deep red. 'If you take your shirt on and off like that without undoing its buttons, they'll all work loose and be lost.'

Garett had been presenting his broad back to her as he surveyed the work in progress. At her words he turned. Heavy, deliberate steps brought him almost too close. Then he bent his head until it was within centimetres of hers, and she could do nothing but stare straight back at him.

'Then I shall simply buy another shirt.' He grinned.

That was enough for Sienna. She had discovered he must be lying to Kane and Molly with his talk of a fictitious yacht, and she was not going to let him charm her out of her anger.

'What with?' she countered.

'Oh, I expect I'll be able to find a few spare coins down behind the cushions of my furniture somewhere.'

He was still highly amused. Sienna blinked, and with an effort remembered Portofino.

'I don't believe you *have* any money, Mr Lazlo,' she said, in a voice like distant thunder. 'You certainly don't have a yacht. I know, because I've been down to Portofino harbour today, and I did some asking around.'

'Ah, well, there's a reason for that.' He was unworried. 'If you were feeling in a curious mood, *signora*, then perhaps you should have started closer to home? For example with that picture of yours hanging over the fireplace.'

'That hideous black thing?'

'Indeed—though now the preliminary results are back, you might try calling it "that previously unknown master-piece" to see if it helps you to like it better.'

'You're joking!'

Garett moved his head slowly and deliberately from side to side. 'The news came through today, while you were out. That picture could very well solve all your problems and more besides. Congratulations.'

Sienna had come so far she could not allow herself to back down now. With a careless flick of her hand she tried to laugh it off.

'Oh? So I suppose you're an international art expert now, as well as a hotshot businessman and fantasy yacht owner?'

'I'm smart enough to know a good thing when I see it, Sienna.'

She got the feeling he was not only talking about the picture. Suddenly her anger was adrift on a restless sea. This man might be an impetuous, arrogant liar—but he was plausible. And quite amazing to look at...

'Then I shall arrange to get a second opinion right away,' she announced.

He closed in on her instantly. 'Are you mad? With all these strangers about, any news like that will travel like lightning. I've been extremely discreet so far. It can stay where it is for the moment—the preliminary identification has been made through photographs. Detailed analysis can wait until the builders get to that room—then the picture will only need to be moved once. It can be taken straight to a secure place for a full assessment.'

'By a *friend* of yours?' Sienna narrowed her eyes.

'By the New York house that deals with all my fine art acquisitions,' he replied smoothly.

'I hope that doesn't mean my picture will be heading off on your fictitious yacht, for some equally remote horizon.'

'Fictitious, eh?' He took her hand in his and led her over to his hire car. Pausing only to wipe a thin layer of bonfire ash from its door handle with a corner of his shirt, he bundled her into the passenger seat. 'Then let me cordially invite you to come and have a taste of my fantasy.'

'Wait! I have to get Imelda's supper ready!' Sienna protested, but without much conviction.

'Let her get it herself for once.' Garett wound the car into a tight turn and roared off down the drive in squeal of tyres. 'It's time you started living for yourself.'

CHAPTER TEN

THEY reached the coast and he jammed the car into a parking space. By the time he opened the passenger door to help Sienna out he was already speaking rapidly into his mobile.

Snapping the phone shut, he pointed out across the harbour. A speedboat was approaching in a froth of sea foam. 'In under two minutes you will be guest of honour on the *Spinifex*. I hope you'll be able to manage a smile when I introduce you to my crew.'

'I still don't believe you,' Sienna persisted, though her hands were damp with uncertainty. 'The *Spinifex* is the biggest yacht in the area, and it is owned by a Canadian billionaire called O'Rourke. I know that because I checked with one of his off-duty deck hands this afternoon.'

Garett laughed, the sound instantly making Sienna feel foolish and silly for jumping to conclusions. 'And how many Europeans can tell the difference between a Canadian and an American accent?'

If Sienna had any doubts about him left, they were whipped away by the launch which collected them a few seconds later.

'I left Manhattan under quite a cloud,' Garett said as they

streaked towards the spectacular ocean-going yacht that was moored not far offshore. 'I had to get away—put some distance between that lifestyle and this. Paying in cash ensures that the only people in Italy who know my real identity are you, Kane, Molly, a couple of businesses and the people who checked my passport.'

'Have you done something illegal in America?' Sienna swallowed nervously.

'No, but perhaps it should be.'

'Immoral?'

'No, although I'm beginning to realise it was hardly moral.'

Sienna could not imagine what he might have done. She looked him up and down cautiously. He was intent on the horizon. The sight of his new ship hardly moved him at all. Sienna could not imagine why it didn't. It was so beautiful, and from the moment Garett helped her aboard she was treated like fine bone china.

After the dusty decrepitude of Aldo's house, the yacht was heaven. It had a sundeck the size of Sienna's kitchen garden, and a staff who could not do enough for her. They treated her as a guest of honour, plying her with canapés and champagne, and as she stood with Garett at the ship's rail, high above the azure waves, she felt like a princess. Standing beside her was the man who was every inch her prince. He was so close she could notice the way his thick dark hair curled at the nape of his neck, and the lighter tone of his skin where his open collar revealed that he did not always work without his shirt. She jumped guiltily the instant he moved to speak, and looked back at the sea to hide her confusion.

'I hope you've got a good appetite for dinner, Sienna.'

'Dinner? But I'm not dressed for it—I've come straight from work.'

'So have I.'

Sienna fingered the lead-crystal glass she was holding. *Now* what was she supposed to do? He had filled her wardrobe with expensive clothes, but she had dressed for a day at the market this morning—not dinner on an ocean-going yacht.

'Oh, dear—I didn't expect this. I would have dressed up for the occasion—'

His dark eyes smiled at her kindly. 'You look all right to me.'

'Are you sure?' Sienna said doubtfully.

'Signora di Imperia, please give me the honour of taking dinner with me this evening—dress entirely optional.' He held out his hand as a gesture of invitation.

Sienna bit her lip. And then she placed her hand in his. She was silent as he escorted her down to the state dining room.

Garett lightened the atmosphere by explaining to her that his unexpected arrival on board had thrown the catering staff into confusion. Sienna would never have guessed. His crew were professional to their fingertips.

Nerves did not ruin her first taste of lobster, and champagne sorbet took away the bitter taste of her shame.

'I'm sorry I ever doubted that you owned the *Spinifex*, Garett,' she murmured after dinner, as he led her away from the dining table on a tour of his new toy.

'Don't worry about it.' He shrugged off her apology, and when he saw the look of unease in her eyes changed the subject to more neutral conversation. 'The workforce at the

Entroterra estate is doing spectacularly well, but I keep my eye on things to make sure everything goes to plan. It makes a terrific change to be on the spot and working in the open air, rather than being cooped up somewhere like this all the time.'

He smiled as he pushed open a russet cherrywood door to show her the sleek interior of an office suite. His comment was tinged with regret, and there was a fleeting bittersweet expression in his eyes.

'You sound as though you aren't looking forward to the end of your holiday project,' she remarked casually.

'There's nothing much left in it for me, is there? Not since you decided to pull back on our arrangement.' There was a devilish glint in his eye.

Sienna darted a look at him. 'So...you really aren't going to keep me to my original promise?'

'No.' He leaned back against the office wall with a heavy sigh. 'There's no pleasure for me in an unwilling partner.'

Sienna wondered how she would have reacted if he'd said he had only suggested the deal on sufferance. 'I have to admit I was nervous.' She looked up at him with worried eyes. 'It is not my sort of thing at all, you see...'

Garett was mystified. How could anyone be nervous when faced with the most pleasurable experience in the world? She had practically signed up for it by herself, in any case— Garett didn't remember giving her any sort of ultimatum. He would certainly never have expected such a shy, retiring girl to agree. When she had taken it on herself to do so, he had known there could be no question of carrying it out. One look into those beautiful, tormented eyes had told him that. How strange it should be that something he looked forward to like paradise filled her with fear. It was unimaginable that any woman should have to force herself to enjoy a night of passion. What must she have been through to make her feel like that?

'Ah, well, it's your choice. But you've denied yourself what would have been a breathtaking experience, Sienna.' He gave her a smile that promised everything but threatened nothing.

Sienna was not so easily persuaded.

'No, I haven't. Sex is nothing but pistons and valves.'

She looked up at him again, and he recognised the pain of memory in her eyes. He recognised it because it stared back at him each morning from his own bathroom mirror.

'Not with me it isn't,' he said softly. 'I could have promised you that, Sienna, believe me.'

'Why should I? Sex has meant nothing but trouble for me in the past. I'm better off without it,' she said in a flat, defeated voice.

'Now, why in the world should you think that?' He had intended the words to sound as dispassionate as hers, but he was unable to hide his annoyance at the man who had spoiled her life.

'All it does is make men angry.'

'No, Sienna, it does not.' He looked deep into her eyes.

'It does. It provokes anger. Anger is what killed Aldo.'

'Your husband died because he got mad at you?'

She nodded. 'I left the telephone flex twisted after making a call. *Again.* What made it worse was the fact that I was ringing the wool shop. Aldo hated me knitting when I should have been running errands. My wilfulness finally sent him over the edge, so the doctor said.'

'The doctor said that? Or was it Imelda?' Garett said slowly. A picture was beginning to form in his mind, and it was not a happy one.

'Imelda told me. Aldo's death certificate gave the cause of his death as a stroke, but Imelda said the doctors were fools, trying to spare my feelings.'

'So…you think you killed your husband?' he probed, watching intently for her reaction to his words.

She nodded. Then shifted in her seat. 'Although some-times…I think…the doctors are probably more likely to be right than…Imelda.' With each hesitation she glanced up at him nervously from beneath her lashes, as though looking for permission to carry on with her awful admission.

'Ahh. I see.'

Garett put the tips of his fingers together and leaned forward in the same way he had faced her at Il Pettirosso.

'I wonder if you would have told me all that before you started standing on your own two feet, organising builders and shopping in Nice, Sienna? And does your hidden streak of rebellion explain why every telephone flex at Entroterra is hopelessly tangled to this day?'

Sienna's head went up. She stared at him for some time. And then she spoke, very slowly and deliberately.

'Yes. I'm very careful to make sure I add a twist to each one every time I use it.'

He held her gaze for a long time. And then he smiled.

'Good. Then there's hope for you yet.'

'What do you mean?'

He answered her question with one of his own.

'Tell me—what exactly do you think would have happened if you and I had gone to bed together, Sienna?'

Her head drooped again. 'You would have lost your temper with me.'

'Never, Sienna. Never in a million years,' he said softly. Seduction was one of the great delights of his life, and he could not stand by and watch anyone throw their life away in celibacy. 'It's the best thing in the world, Sienna.'

He smiled, watching her consider this. It was like seeing a non-swimmer trying to convince themselves they would like to drown. Nothing short of a truly mad impulse was going to save this situation. Garett could not bear to think of such a lovely girl being lost to love. 'Look, why don't you give yourself the luxury of drafting yourself a new agreement, Sienna?'

She shook her head miserably. But as she looked up at him he could see that his words had tempted her. There was intrigue as well as hesitancy in her eyes.

'The work on your villa will be finished within a few weeks. Then perhaps the two of us can have a celebratory toast. On that night you can decide if you want to take things further—to find out what delights life can hold. Does that sound good to you?'

Sienna nodded, but did not move.

'And now you can forget all about it until and unless you fancy taking advantage of that offer. It's your choice, Sienna.' He looked down at her and tucked a wayward strand of hair behind her ear. Sienna shivered, but she wasn't cold at all.

When she refused to meet his eyes it was because of guilt rather than fear. She had been a willing partner in every touch and every kiss they had shared. A more than willing partner, if she was to be truthful. Now, the power lay in her own hands to cross that invisible line dividing irresistible Garett from terrifying Aldo. Garett was giving her that choice.

She shook her head slowly. 'Why should a man like you, with all your advantages in life, be bothered about somebody like me? You could have anyone you want, whenever you want them.' Sienna sighed, finally putting her chronic lack of self-esteem into words.

He strolled around to the front of his desk and sat down on it, one leg swinging. 'Sienna, something happened to me a short time ago which made me want to outgrow that lifestyle. The more I look about me now, the more I think I should enjoy what I have and not worry about amassing more and more "stuff". I'd lost sight of what was important in life. I only began to realise my mistake when I found myself sounding off at a little urchin who was a mirror image of me at the same age. Like him, I lost my mother early in life and had to live on the streets. I had no right to consider myself any better than he was. I simply escaped by making my own luck. That's the only difference between us.'

'Oh, Garett…' Sienna gasped, staring at him wide-eyed. Suddenly she lost all her fear. It was all she could do to resist throwing herself into his arms. The emotion scared her. She had never felt like that before about anyone or anything— particularly not a man. 'What happened to you?'

'My drunken father beat my mother to death because she couldn't stop me crying.'

Sienna looked him straight in the eyes. The expression there warned her that any offer of sympathy would be quickly brushed aside.

He stood a little straighter, and his voice held a note of shock when he spoke again. 'Do you know, I've never told anyone that before?'

The way he discounted his tragedy with an easy laugh did not fool Sienna for a second.

'What on earth became of you?'

'I was very quiet after that.'

He stood up and walked over to a cupboard. There, he took out a bottle of champagne and some glasses. Silently, he poured them each a small measure and handed one to her.

'And yet you still drink?'

'Champagne doesn't have the kick of homemade liquor. And I am always careful to pace myself. Social drinking is fine. I don't need to get drunk to have fun. I've got all the entertainment any man could ever need right here on board the *Spinifex*. Computers, cinema, top-quality sound systems everywhere—even in there...' He gestured to one of the smoke-coloured walls of his office. At the flick of a switch the glass cleared, and she was looking into a fully-fitted executive gym. He saluted her with his champagne flute. 'In fact I could up-anchor right now and live the rest of my life without ever setting foot on shore again. I could become a water-gypsy, travelling the Seven Seas.'

'And will you?'

'Don't worry. I'm not going anywhere before I've completed the Entroterra project. And then who knows? It might be the Southern Ocean—although to be perfectly honest it won't be long before I start hankering for the offices of Lazlo, Manhattan, again. I'm expecting my console fingers to start twitching at any moment.'

'You have all this, and yet you still want to go back to the city?' Sienna shook her head, amazed.

'Not yet—although, as I say, it can't be long before I get the urge. The longest I've been away from the office in the past was when my appendix got tired of being ignored and I developed peritonitis. Even then I had my staff smuggle work into my hospital suite as soon as I was fit to hold a pen.'

Sienna gazed at him. 'But you tell *me* to slow down and chill out!'

'You know what they say: "those who can, do—those who can't, teach". I've had dozens of health professionals of one sort or another on my case for years. The aquarium, the relaxing recordings, the ambient lighting, the exercise regimes—they've tried all those techniques and it's all been a total waste of time. I'm completely immune. Nothing works on me. I like to work.' He shrugged, leaving his words hanging in the air.

Sienna's brow wrinkled in thought, but only for an instant. 'There must be something that could help you to unwind,' she said slowly—then caught sight of the clock. 'Look at the time! I must go—I need to get back for Imelda.' She jumped up.

'I keep telling you—let her look after herself,' Garett said, but he made no real attempt to stop her. Instead he turned away.

He reached for his jacket, when Sienna might have expected him to criticise her desperate need to run according to someone else's timetable. The only comment he made was when he dropped her off outside the villa.

He came around and opened the car door for her, and

she darted out immediately. 'Don't be in such a hurry. Anyone would think you were trying to escape from me!' He observed dryly as he closed her door.

Sienna *was* keen to get inside—but not to get away from Garett. In fact the opposite was true. She almost found the nerve to give him a peck on the cheek as she thanked him for the spontaneous evening they had shared, but backed away at the last moment and ducked inside the house. There, she raced upstairs to watch the lights of Garett's car disappearing down the drive. She had discovered the secret of his past. Now an idea was forming in her mind. It *was* true that she needed to attend to Imelda—but her stepmother was not the main reason Sienna had wanted to get home. She intended that tomorrow would be a busy day. Her alarm clock was going to be waking her before first light. She needed to get some sleep.

Garett arrived on foot next morning. Now that the fences were all repaired and painted gleaming white, he enjoyed the walk. Dressed in his working clothes of casual shirt and jeans, he swung along the lane between the Bradleys' house and Sienna's villa. The summer was being kind. Dry, clear days allowed the workmen to get on at speed.

Swallows were skimming over the hazel grove as he walked between the coppiced stumps. He stopped and watched them for a few minutes. Sienna had shown him their nests in the hayloft, where the birds returned each spring. It would be well into the autumn before their final chicks were fledged. He had postponed renovating the building where they nested without telling Sienna he would probably have left Italy before the work started. Like the swallows, he would be on the move soon enough.

For once in his life the idea made him feel uncomfortable. Garett was in no hurry to see this project come to an end. He was growing more reluctant with each passing day, and it was the only time he could remember being in such a situation. The problem is Sienna, he thought. At first she had been nothing but a beautiful distraction. Then gradually he had learned of the sadness hiding behind her beautiful eyes. Until his arrival, everyone had bullied her. Now, she was discovering confidence in her own abilities. Within the past couple of days she had even suggested making a start on some of the redundant farm buildings outside of the first phase of redevelopment. She wanted to turn them into holiday homes. Tourism would help the whole area, not just the Entroterra estate.

Garett hoped he could put some of her plans into place for her before he got the urge to leave. At least then he would have the satisfaction of leaving her a potential business with firm foundations, which she could develop after he was gone. He gritted his teeth and faced a grim reality. She might struggle to survive without him. He would certainly worry about her—or at least spare her a thought now and then, he corrected himself. She was finding more and more determination by the day, but she would need it. He wondered how he would eventually find the words to tell her his work was finished and he was leaving. His fists clenched at the thought, and he was surprised to find how uncomfortable and unnatural the action felt to him now. If he was a two-legged rat he would just up-anchor one day and disappear over the horizon.

That would be the quick, clean way to go. But it would also be the act of a coward. And he could never be accused of being one of those.

Despite the depth of his concentration, Garett became aware of irregular sounds bouncing across the valley towards him. Someone was using a sledgehammer. The sound echoed through the peaceful hazel grove like the mating racket of a trainee woodpecker. It was too early for any of the men to be at work yet. As he reached the villa, everything fell still and silent. He strode around to the kitchen, looking for Sienna, but he could not find her. She was not anywhere on the ground floor of the villa. He went back out into the yard just as the inexpert thumping started up again. It was coming from the range of sheds Sienna wanted to turn into holiday homes. She must have got her man Ermanno on the job, he thought grimly. Why couldn't everyone wait for him to arrive and take control?

A fine cloud of dust rose lazily through the still air, glowing in the early-morning sunlight. He wrenched open the cowshed doors, ready to give the hired help a piece of his mind.

Instead of meeting Ermanno, he came face to face with Sienna. She was alone in the byre, all wide-eyed innocence and streaked with dust. Seeing him, she dropped the enormous sledgehammer she was holding with a great gasp of relief. Garett strode forward.

'What in the world are you doing, Sienna?'

She scuffed one toe across the plaster-dusted cobble-stones. 'Well…you are all so busy with everything else, but the idea of doing something for myself really appealed to me. Restoring this range of buildings must be right down at the bottom of your list of priorities, so thought I'd make a start alone.'

'What on? Killing yourself? How do you know you aren't going to bring the whole place down on your head by attacking it like this?'

'Because your notes have all the supporting walls marked in red, and this one is drawn in blue,' she said simply, holding out a copy of his own document towards him as proof. 'See?'

'Perhaps I'd better take charge of that.' Garett's expression was almost as dark as the barn. 'Where is your man Ermanno? Has he gone out of his mind, letting you run riot like this?'

'Ermanno has a bad back. I sent him out to bring the goats in, instead. He can manage that.'

'I'd rather you didn't take on heavy work like this.' Garett put down the toolbox he had brought with him. After a moment's consideration he took the hammer from her. 'This job needs strength.'

He tightened his fingers on the shaft of the hammer, feeling its weight and substance. This was real man's work. He flexed all his muscles, ripples of power coursing through his body. If only he could have had an outlet like this the day of his crime on Wall Street. That little boy's face haunted him still. All he'd done was beg for quarters, and Garett had rounded on him in fury. It had been the last straw at the end of a frantic day full of deadlines, a busy week packed with demands, and the never-ending pressure of business with no hope of a break—

His outburst had been so loud, so terrible, that hard-faced pedestrians had almost stopped to stare. The crowds had parted around them, leaving Garett's towering rage pinning the tiny boy beneath his tirade. That was the moment, the second, the heartbeat, when Garett had realised he had to get away. He had turned and marched straight to the airport, hardly caring where he went so long as it was completely outside the orbit of Planet Business.

And now here he was, working again. The difference was that he had left all the traffic, burger fumes and bustle far behind. Here, birdsong, warm breezes, and the perfume of roses from the garden surrounded him. Best of all, the most beautiful woman in the world was looking on. This was the sort of work he liked.

CHAPTER ELEVEN

'STAND well back, Sienna.'

Always obedient, she did as she was told. Sliding one hand down the wooden shaft to test its weight again, Garett considered. Hefting the weapon once, twice, and then a third time, he took an almighty swing at the wall. The hammer's head smashed into the plaster. Garett's arms absorbed the shockwaves effortlessly, and he blew a cloud of dust out of his face. Sienna's face was a study. She was impressed, and he responded.

'How's that?' He raised a brow nonchalantly in mock arrogance. She laughed.

'You've done more with one blow than I managed with all my pecking.'

'Shall I carry on?'

They both knew the answer to that.

Garett took a deep breath, and attacked the wall again. Wielding the hammer produced a lot of dust—and the realisation that he had wasted God knew how many years sitting behind a desk when he might have been doing something useful like this. Inspired, he threw three more massive blows at the masonry. It began to crumble.

Within minutes his shirt was wet with sweat, and both he and Sienna were breathless with laughter. Stopping to strip off, he laid bare the body that Sienna had been dreaming about.

'This is tremendous therapy.'

His glistening chest rose and fell in a way that stirred Sienna as surely as feeling his hands working over her body had done.

'That's what I thought. I know exactly how you feel.'

'No.' He shook his head, laughing as droplets of perspiration flew from his tousled hair. 'You can't begin to imagine. It's giving me such satisfaction to throw all my energy into a violent act like this. I'm working out frustrations I didn't know I had.'

'I knew.' Sienna's lips parted. It was only a small smile, but there was no mistaking the major triumph she was trying to hide.

'No.' He dropped the head of the sledgehammer on the cobblestone floor with a hollow thud. 'How could a quiet, retiring girl like you ever know what demons were hiding inside me?'

'You didn't see what this wall looked like before I started work.' She laughed. Crouching down in the wreckage, she began pulling the smashed spars and lumps of plaster around, fitting them back together. There were chalk marks scrawled on them, he noticed. Then, as he watched, Sienna's jigsaw began to make sense. Soon it revealed two inexpert portraits in white chalk.

'There! Imelda and Aldo.'

'Not very flattering likenesses.' He leaned on the hammer and smiled. 'Now, why don't you go inside and fetch us some drinks? You don't want to get involved in dirty work like this.'

But *I* do, Garett thought, enjoying the benefits of physical labour for the first time.

He lifted the hammer again, testing the shaft as though testing himself against its weight. Sienna revelled in the sight of all that power contained within his muscular torso. It deserved far more than the soft drinks and fast food her other workmen enjoyed. While he went back to demolishing the partition, Sienna returned to her kitchen—as soon as she could tear her eyes away from his body.

Garett eventually delegated the job to workmen—but only when he had burned off a lot of stress. It powered him with a new enthusiasm for the rest of the project. At midday, Sienna brought a picnic out from the house for him. Before eating, he washed in a bucket of ice-cold water at the well.

Sienna spread out a blanket beneath the lemon shelter, but her mind was not on her work. She was distracted by the backlit image of Garett, showering drops of glittering sunshine. As he strolled back across the courtyard, he ran his work-shirt over his chest, then around and beneath his arms. Sienna jumped to her feet.

'I'll fetch you a towel—'

'There's no need. There. It's done.' Pulling the shirt on again, he dropped down to sit opposite her. The airy conservatory held only the faintest tang of new paint, but this was quickly masked when she cut into the pie she had brought.

'That smells good,' he murmured appreciatively. Leaning forward to inspect the filling, he showered both the calzone and Sienna with droplets of water.

'Your hair is soaking!' She laughed, flapping her hand at him.

Immediately he leaned back. What surprised her was that he did it with a laugh. It was a reaction Sienna never normally experienced when she asked someone to do something, so she giggled, too.

'You should do that more often, Sienna. Smiling suits you.'

She blinked at him. It was a compliment, but this time it had nothing to do with trying to get her into bed. Garett was not even bothering to check on the result of his words. Instead, he was attacking her cooking as though there was a danger someone might take it away from him. He was *not* complaining that she had saved time and effort by making one large calzone instead of several smaller ones. Unlike Aldo, Garett never once mentioned dyspepsia, acid reflux, indigestion, oxalic acid levels or dairy and wheat intolerance.

While Sienna marvelled at this busily contented silence, Garett picked up the knife she had put down and carved himself a second man-sized chunk of pie. She gasped.

More than half of it was gone already, and his appetite showed no signs of slowing down.

'What's the matter?'

'N-nothing.' Sienna tried not to look too hungry as she eyed the remaining calzone.

'Aren't you having any?'

'Only when you are sure you've finished.'

He stopped eating and looked at her strangely. Then he jammed the knife through the portion he was about to start eating. Scraping half onto the second plate she had brought, he pushed it towards her.

'You don't honestly think I'd only let you eat when I've finished?' He was shocked, and his reaction surprised Sienna.

'It's what I'm used to.'

He let out his breath in a thin stream.

'That is *not* the way I do things.'

This time Sienna smiled at him in a way he had never seen anyone smile before—man, woman or business associate. In the time it took him to recognise gratitude, she had picked up the pitcher of lemonade she'd carried out from the kitchen. Garett guessed what was coming next. Before she could pour him a glass, his hand closed over hers.

'I'll do it.'

Putting down his plate, he reached for a tumbler and filled it to the brim. Then he handed it to her.

'Go on—take it.'

Sienna accepted it with another welcome smile. Garett did not return to his meal immediately. He waited until she started to eat. Only when he was sure she was catering for herself as well as for him did he pick up his fork again. A warm glow of satisfaction brought genuine expression to his lips. He had been so busy with the Entroterra estate that there had been no time to dwell on his own feelings before now. Now he felt fit and fulfilled in a way he had never known, and in a better state to put everyone else's world to rights, too.

It must be the weather—and the enforced absence of a computer link with his international offices.

'I'm sorry you didn't believe I owned the *Spinifex,* Sienna,' he said eventually, when the edges had been knocked off his hunger. 'But I had my reasons for arriving here undercover. I wanted to get away—to put some distance between the office and me. My staff would have tracked me down in seconds if I'd been entirely truthful everywhere. Do you believe in me now?'

They looked at each other. Garett usually hid his true feelings, but today he could only hope Sienna's expression was not mirroring his own. She looked as amazed as he felt. As her features became troubled, he risked another question.

'You don't look very sure?'

She put down her cutlery. One finger rubbed absently across her brow. 'Well…if you want the truth…I'm still a bit worried about things. Whether it is quite right to sell that big painting, for a start…'

'What's the worst that can happen? Some dusty old museum buys it for a healthy sum and you never have to worry about money again. Where's the harm in that? You're *minus* one monstrosity, and *plus* one small fortune.' He gave her a quick smile, but as he glanced at her it dissolved into a frown. 'What's the matter? Have you got a headache, Sienna?'

'Yes. How did you know?'

'Something about the way you're currently rubbing a hole in your forehead gave it away. Here.' He reached into the pocket of his jeans and pulled out a small plastic case. He handed it to her. Opening it, she found sealed blisters of painkillers. Garett was already pouring her a glass of mineral water.

'I'm an expert in stress headaches—though it's been weeks since I've needed any of these tablets myself. A couple of them and you'll improve quite soon. Although to speed things up…'

He moved around until he was kneeling behind her on the picnic rug. Placing his hands lightly on her shoulders, he began easing her taut muscles, untying all the knots that Aldo and Imelda and shyness and worry and debt had tied.

Sienna allowed herself to do the impossible. She leaned against his hands and sighed.

Garett had expected her to resist. Her willing consent gave him something to think about. Did she realise how he ached for her body? How he had been purposely denying himself for his own selfish reasons? Because he wanted a break from women as much as he needed one from work? Watching her grimace as she took the painkillers, he wondered which of them was suffering most. He certainly wasn't. It had been ages since he'd last checked into the office computer system to see how things were going. Until recently an enforced break like this would have had him climbing the walls. But Garett was beginning to realise he did not need work as much as it needed him.

'Now you've finished your medicine, lean back against the wall and relax,' he murmured, leaning forward to take her glass.

'I can't really get comfortable, sitting here.'

'Close your eyes, and try.'

Alert to every sound, Sienna heard him moving around in front of her. Then she felt him catch up her wrist. The next moment he was working magic. He started to massage the back of her hand with slow, sure movements. Millimetre by millimetre the pressure of his thumbs worked in concert over her thin, delicate skin. Tiny circling movements worked at the tension, smoothing and kneading it all away. For minutes on end she sat transfixed by the feel of his touch, hypnotised by the distant sound of a robin's song fluting over from the hazel coppice. She could not move, but she did not want to. Garett was in charge. Reaching her fingers, he manipulated each one, working over them to warm and free the frozen muscles. It was the first time in her adult life that anyone had ever done anything so personal, just for her. When he finally finished working over her little finger and his touch fell away, she sighed.

'Your fingers were as inflexible as a fistful of birch twigs. You must learn to let go, Sienna.' His voice drifted through the warm, rose-perfumed air.

'Oh, it would be nice.'

There was real longing in her voice. She felt him move around in front of her again. If only this pampering could go on for ever…

With a gasp, she felt him lift her other hand. Her eyes flew open and met with his. For long moments they gazed at each other. Sienna could feel the embers of her desire stirring beneath his steady gaze, but she did not dare make any move or sound which might make him reconsider, change his mind and stop.

'Do you want me to carry on, or not?' His voice was husky, almost challenging. Obediently she lowered her lashes again. This time, though, she did not entirely close her eyes. She made sure she could see enough to watch him continue the massage. The sight of his long, strong fingers at work was almost as much of a distraction as the warmth of his nearness.

'This is wonderful,' she breathed at last.

'Of course it is. Every woman deserves pampering, and you more than most, Sienna.'

'Molly was right. You really do have a silver tongue.'

He smiled, straight into her eyes. Sienna's lips parted. Already her body was warming in response to the closeness of him. His touch on her wrist made her painfully aware of a thudding pulse, but to whom it belonged—him, her, either or both—Sienna was powerless to know. She trembled, and in response his hands slid up her arms, moulding her body to his will as he drew her gently towards his body.

'I can read the mind of every woman I meet,' he breathed, resting his face lightly against the sleek luxuriance of her hair. 'Every woman loves pleasure—and I am the man to give it to you, Sienna.'

Her heart rose. Breathless and dizzy, she could not resist when his mouth closed on hers, kissing away all her doubts.

'Please…no. We shouldn't. This isn't decent…' she gasped, with a total lack of credibility. The waterfall of desire that was powering through her body was washing away any will-power she might possess. Garett had fascinated her from the moment they first met. Tortured by guilt then, Sienna had read lust in his every smile. Whenever they'd made physical contact by accident—the brush of fingers over that spilled glass of wine, their creation of the stracchi—she had thought it was the ultimate high. But this…this was so right, so unlike anything she had experienced before, that nothing could stop her now.

'Oh, it can get a lot more indecent than this, believe me,' he breathed, his lips parted in a smile that was at once triumphant and expectant. 'It will become as indecent as you want it, Sienna. No more and no less. When you are ready, I am going to pleasure you in a way that you will never forget.'

He stood up, drawing her to her feet as well. Then he allowed his fingers to trail down her arm until he could enclose her hand with his.

'Come with me... Have you seen the Entroterra's master suite now that the interior designers have finished?' He threw a smile over his shoulder.

'Garett...I can't...'

'Why not?'

She did not know. Every touch of his hand, each look, drew her closer to Garett and widened the yawning chasm between her experiences with him and with Aldo. She could barely remember the dead days of her marriage. All that existed was the warm anticipation of Garett's body.

She was almost delirious with expectation as he led her through the house that he had transformed into a home for her. When they reached the polished oak door of the master suite, he took a key from his pocket and unlocked it. The door swung open silently, revealing a reception room with thick, soft carpet and opulent furnishings. The suite was so muffled with fine damasks and silks that Sienna knew they would be completely cocooned in luxurious privacy. Garett stepped forward.

She hesitated one last time on the threshold, leaning back against the steady pressure of his hand.

'I can't. Not here...'

'It is the ideal place. We are behind locked doors...' He clicked the catch and his milk chocolate eyes smiled their slow, seductive smile.

'It isn't that.'

He let go of her hand.

'Garett...' She swallowed hard, moistening her lips with

the tip of her tongue. It was an action he clearly found fascinating, which didn't make it any easier for Sienna to continue. 'Is it true that you really do have—what did Molly call it?—a girl in every port?'

He laughed, touched by her innocence. 'Molly does me a disservice.' He smiled roguishly. 'In my time I've had girls in practically every port, city, prairie and valley throughout the civilised world. And parts of the uncivilised world too,' he added with a wink. 'It would be cruel to disappoint any of the lovely ladies of my acquaintance.'

'Do you remember them all?'

'But of course.'

He watched her for a moment, seeing the first flush of lust fade from her skin. It looked as though he was losing her.

'It all depends what a woman wants from a relationship,' he said.

Sienna's face worked through several emotions, until she could manage to put her fear into words.

'I couldn't bear to fall in love with a man like you,' she said carefully.

Ah. Garett allowed himself a small, playful smile. 'Who said anything about love?'

He saw her shoulders soften with relief. He had been right. That was it.

'You mean, Sienna, that you might like to try a taste of afternoon delight without any strings attached?'

'I wouldn't put it quite like that. It's just that…I want to know what I've been missing, but I can't bear being hurt.'

There spoke a woman after his own heart—though not the business about being hurt, of course. Garett had developed armour plating at the age of six. There wasn't a woman alive who could get through that, he was sure. His mother was dead, and he had seen it happen. That was why he was determined to treat women in the way they deserved, with generosity, expertise and fun—because Gilda Lazlo had never known anything like that in her short, miserable life. Her son had spent his own life trying to make up for that. It was a challenge to which he was perfectly suited, in body, mind and spirit.

'So…if we were to…' She looked away, embarrassed. 'You wouldn't tell anyone about it, Garett? Not Kane, or Molly, or anyone at all?'

'No, of course not. That is not the action of a gentleman.'

They looked at each other for long moments. Then Sienna made a tiny movement toward him. Before she could change her mind he was there, taking her in his arms again.

'What will everyone say if they find out?'

'They aren't going to find out. Nobody will ever know. And if they did, they'd all wonder what took you so long.'

'Even Imelda?'

'Imelda will be green with envy.'

Sienna put her hands on his shoulders and levered herself out of his grasp long enough to give him a look of amused astonishment.

'You really think a lot of yourself, don't you, Mr Garett Lazlo?'

'I have to, or nobody else will,' he said succinctly, his eyes on her lips. 'Now, let's have no more talking.'

He kissed her, pushing his fingers through the tangle of her hair to draw her near, cupping her shoulders. His every movement urged her to snuggle closer. Marriage had taught Sienna to see sex in terms of duty, not lust. When Garett responded to her tentative hands it was with a speed that took her breath away. She felt his taut muscles glide under the smooth golden skin, with well-practised economical movements. His touch was already moving over her top, pulling it down to expose the thin flesh-coloured bra beneath. Those actions gave her such a rush of adrenaline that her own fingers went to the buttons of his shirt, desperate to expose his warm, perfect skin. Peeling the white cotton away from his shoulders, she was entranced once again by the dusting of dark hair across the taut perfection of his chest.

'Two can play at that game.' He leaned forward, simul-taneously removing her top and burying his face against the fluid curve of her shoulder. Sexual electricity crackled through her, as brutal as the rasp of his cheek against her delicate skin.

'I need a shave.' He looked down with wicked amuse-ment. Her creamy white shoulder was pink with the pressure from his slightly roughened chin. It was a physical manifestation of his masculinity, and it gave her an extra tingle of pleasure.

'It doesn't matter,' Sienna breathed, closing her eyes. She was being transported to a totally different world. This was all so different from her previous experiences of sex. She wanted everything to be new and exciting, to touch and be touched in ways that would have been unthinkable during her life with Aldo. Her *half*-life, she realised, as Garett's hands swept over her back and dived into the waistband of her skirt.

They were still standing up, and this was broad daylight. Intimacy for Garett was clearly not some brief embarrassment, to be hidden away in the darkness of night. He was relishing every moment. She could see it in the clear, untroubled planes of his face, and in his eyes, half closed, but still watching her from beneath those long dark, lashes. He intended her to enjoy the sensation, too.

With practised movements he removed her skirt. His long, strong fingers were massaging her bottom through the thin fabric of her silk panties. Slowly, dreamily, she began moving in response to his touch: pushing herself against the resistance of his hands. As he drew his teeth across her throat, sending shiver after shiver of pleasure streaming through her body, his thumbs hooked into the flimsy ties at the sides of her briefs. When she realised what he was doing, Sienna wriggled with pleasure. The movement helped him to release the ribbons. With a gasp she felt the insubstantial triangles of lace fall away. Before she could pull back in alarm his hands returned to her shoulders, pulling her into a kiss that made the world fall away.

'Garett…' she breathed, as his lips moved across her cheek to taste the outline of her ear.

'I know.'

Lifting her off her feet, he strode across the salon. Kicking open the bedroom door, he took her inside. But the force he had used to enter frightened her. Feeling her go rigid in his arms, he stopped and looked at her sharply.

'If you are having second thoughts, Sienna, now is the time to call a halt.'

'You would do that for me?'

'I would do it for any woman.'

She watched his face minutely. 'Despite the way you opened that door?'

'What? Oh, Sienna.' He laughed. "To put you down and use my hand on the latch would have ruined the moment. Rather like conversation,' he finished pointedly.

Tentatively, Sienna lifted a hand to his hair. Savouring the feel of the fine, dense darkness, she moved her fingers upward until her palm was close to his ear.

'And has it?'

In response he moved his head to lean gently against her hand. 'No, Sienna. No, it has not…' His voice was low and rough, as though he was not used to whispering. 'Tell me how much you want me.'

She closed her eyes. There was no time for speech. Her lips parted as a small moan of anticipation escaped. He did not need any more encouragement. Tossing her lightly onto the bed, he followed her with the predatory grace of a panther. She felt herself quail beneath the towering masculinity of his need—but only for an instant. As he took her mouth with an urgent kiss of possession she felt a shockwave of desire sear through her whole body. Engulfing her with his arms, he pulled her into a savage embrace. He was an irresistible force. She absorbed it with a frisson of fear tipped with excitement. She was powerless to resist. He assaulted all her senses at once. The warm, sweet fragrance of his masculinity, the pressure of his body against hers, the sound of her name on his lips… She was a petal, tumbled and teased and overwhelmed by the hurricane of his desire.

The shadow of him moved over her like a cloud. She closed her eyes, blinded by pleasure as his mouth sought hers. His tongue was a dagger of desire, thrusting into her mouth as he kissed, kissed and kissed again. Roving over her body with his hands, he was eager to sample delight. She felt the tiny abrasions as his work-hardened hands slid over her silky skin to cup the fullness of her breasts. His thumbs moved in circles, tantalising her nipples into rigid peaks. Her whole body began to rise, synchronised with his rhythmic movements. The friction of his arousal excited her still more, until uncontrollable cries of longing stole all the breath from her body. Over and over she pleaded for a release from the temptation that had burned within her since their first meeting.

'Wait…I want to make this last—for both of us.'

He held his body taut against the soft appeal of hers. Desire for her had almost robbed him of control, but he never allowed anything to spoil his pleasure.

'Garett…' she called to him softly, pleading with her eyes. They were large and dark with unspoken promise. 'I've waited so long for this moment… Oh, Garett, I want you so badly…'

'You can have everything you want. Just reach out. There are no limits…'

His breath escaped in a low throb of desire. She would never know how tight a curb he had been keeping on his own libido since he had first seen her, first imagined her here in bed, in his arms and in his power… The reality was even better than his wildest fantasies. There was nothing to compare with the sweet softness of Sienna's skin beneath his fingers, the texture of her nipples against his tongue and the undiluted tang of rosewater on her skin. The pleasure was so intense it was all he could do to stop himself plunging into her straight away, sinking to the hilt in the warm, welcoming depth he had imagined so vividly.

His heart was racing. Any moment now he was going to gain the ultimate prize.

Sienna's hands clenched on his shoulders. She could hear her breath sighing. As long as she could take him with her—all the way—she was ready to plunge off this precipice of desire…

'I've never felt like this before,' she gasped. 'Oh, Garett…love me…'

They coupled and tumbled all afternoon and long into the night. Garett filled her body, mind and senses with absolute rapture. All memory of her cold, lonely marriage evaporated like frost in sunlight. They moved through dreams of cotton sheets and flickering firelight. Sienna could not remember falling asleep. Only the lightness of his fingers as they traced over the smooth, soft skin of her thigh…

She drifted into the next day through a haze of warmth and perfume. For long moments she lay still and silent, hoping not to disturb him. It had been a hot, heady night. Lying on her side like this, she could see straight out of the open French doors leading onto the master bedroom's balcony. The sun was a ripe peach, hanging over the pine ridge. It was just waiting to be enjoyed to the full.

Sienna relished the silence for a few moments more, wondering what they might get up to with a whole summer day stretching ahead of them. The builders were practically finished on the estate. Garett would not be needed for work. She could keep him trapped within her arms for as long as she liked. The idea of his long, strong limbs tangling with hers again began to arouse her fully from sleep. Lazily, she stretched out in the bed, intending to stroke him with her instep. She reached, and then rolled over to find him in their enormous playground—but he was not there. The bed was empty. She ran her hands over the tumbled sheets. They were as cold as only cotton could be.

Sitting up, she listened for any sounds coming through from the adjoining bathroom. There was absolute silence.

'Garett?'

Sliding out of bed, she grabbed her negligee and, barefoot, started off across the bedroom. Billowing silk and lace around her shoulders, she pushed open the *en suite* bathroom door and went in. The marble floor was cool and welcoming, but the room was empty. She went through the door leading directly from the wet-room into the dressing room beyond. That was empty, too.

'Garett?'

The windows on this side of the house were closed. Looking down onto the courtyard, she saw that his ice-blue hire-car was gone.

Don't panic, she told herself. That's the first thing the old Sienna would have done. There are a million reasons why he is not here. He might have gone out to fetch a newspaper, or a surprise breakfast from the village.

Then she thought of the internet news he accessed in his site office each morning. He had no need to visit the shops. And his instructions to Sienna about spending freely but wisely had extended to grocery deliveries. To save her time and stress, everything was brought right to the door. She knew that fresh orange juice and pastries would be waiting downstairs for her right now.

Where was Garett? What could he possibly need?

It would have been the act of a desperate woman to rush

outside and interrogate the first builder she met. Sienna was desperate, but discretion was ingrained in her. She forced herself to shower and dress before going downstairs. She was still pulling a brush through her hair as she dashed into the small salon leading from the villa's great hall. Garett had transferred his site office from the Bradleys' villa the moment there had been a decent space on site.

She walked around the desk to see if it held any clues to his disappearance. A screensaver of the *Spinifex* cut across the blank screen. She hit a key at random and found herself staring at his computer's calendar. Garett was meticulous in all things. Every delivery, each appointment for the Entroterra project was logged by date and time. He never left anything to chance. She could track everything—right through to the projected completion date. Sienna studied each day, but there was nothing to suggest any problem or appointment that would drag him away from her bed.

With growing panic she thought back over those past few frantic hours. Two memories—one bitter, one sweet—collided in her mind. She remembered the remark he had made, as light as air, that he could leave at any minute, ready to take up the carefree life of a water gypsy. And as his voice echoed across the emptiness, she heard herself calling out to him through the shadows of night: *'Love me, Garett, I love you so much…'*

She had felt him draw back at the time—only minutely, but the movement had definitely been there.

Sienna covered her face with her hands. What had she done? Of all the things to say to a free spirit like Garett, whose life was so different from her own that she could not begin to understand him. A declaration like that must have been poison to him. He had obviously waited until she'd fallen asleep and then left her.

Ice water ran through her veins. She thought desperately of where he might go. Perhaps he had stopped by to pick up his things from the Bradleys'. Before she could think of ringing them, a warning message flashed up on the computer screen in front of her. It was a list of meetings based in New York. The first was to happen in fewer than eighteen hours, and after that the calendar was divided up into time slots and notes, all referring to Garett.

Her words of love must have been too much, and he had thrown himself back into work. She was sure of it. As she watched, the screen refreshed itself again. This time it was with confirmation that a single first-class flight to New York had been booked in Garett's name.

It was a one-way ticket.

CHAPTER TWELVE

IT WAS a long time before Sienna got up from the computer screen. She was red-eyed and resigned. There was no point in chasing after him. Instinctively she had always known this would happen, but now she was faced with the agonising reality. Garett was a free agent. He had never made any secret about that. Now he had made the decision to go. But he had torn out her heart and taken it with him. She walked slowly out into the kitchen, trying to come to terms with what had happened.

When she opened her brand-new maximum efficiency fridge, the flood of cold air brought her to her senses. Her whole life had been spent living in the past—until Garett arrived. He had taught her to look forward to the future, not back. She had made a monumental mistake in opening up to him, and he had acted completely in character. He had taken action, and moved on. Sienna realised that was what *she* must do now. There were final arrangements to be made with the builders and landscapers working around her estate. It was nothing she could not handle, fired by the confidence Garett had inspired in her.

But Sienna did not feel inspired. She felt small,

abandoned and alone. She poured herself a long, cold glass of fresh orange juice. Then she put two croissants to warm and went to look for the organic chocolate spread.

She moved around her sparkling new kitchen in a daze. Plates were rattled and cutlery was dropped instead of being placed. She hardly knew what she was doing. The warm bouquet of hot, buttery pastry and freshly ground coffee only added to her misery. They were all things that Garett had brought her. Now she had ruined everything by saying the one thing a man like that never wanted to hear. Abandonment was no more than she should have expected. His awful childhood must have damaged him, planted something wayward in his nature. After all, he had told her about those legions of girls in his past. And it was no more than Molly had joked about.

Working on automatic, Sienna loaded her croissants with chocolate spread.

Yes, she realised slowly, Garett brought all this into my life. But he never *bought* it, she reminded herself. She had kept her integrity right to the end. She had only slept with him when she wanted to—not because it had been part of some bargain. The authenticated painting meant she would be able to hold on to her honour independently, too.

Piling her tray with the pastries, the glass of juice and a foaming cappuccino, she headed back to Garett's office to call up the Lazlo, Manhattan, website.

What she read there confirmed all her worst fears. A newsflash announced that the boss was back in command after his unscheduled break.

That was all it had ever been, Sienna told herself: a beautiful, temporary dream. She closed her eyes, reliving every touch, every kiss, each burning moment of searing passion they had shared. Then a call from somewhere far away, from Imelda's suite, reminded her that she was on her own again. Or at least she would be—if she could find that inner strength Garett had always talked about. She opened her eyes and stared down at her abandoned breakfast. Then she came to a decision. She picked up the telephone.

Garett Lazlo had certainly made things happen on the Entroterra estate. But Sienna had started to realise she could do that, too. The changes around this place had only just begun. She would see to that.

Garett began regretting his action the instant he eased his way from beneath Sienna's sleeping body. His pride kept telling him it was for the best. She had told him she loved him, and any woman who made that sort of claim meant nothing but trouble. He knew that from bitter experience. Work was the only worthwhile mistress, his inner voice repeated, over and over again.

Now, he strode through airports and subway stations, oblivious to the packs of photographers and journalists who hunted him all the way back to his office. The racket was phenomenal. It crushed in on him like a pain. He had forgotten just how loud New York City was. It was as different from the peace and beauty of Entroterra as Sienna's *latte* was from instant coffee.

That thought worked like aversion therapy as a secretary greeted him with a cup of double-decaffeinated, as prescribed by his healthcare team. He grimaced, and handed it straight over to the girl who introduced herself as his new PA. Within thirty seconds Garett was yearning for Sienna's soft lilt, and the prospect of her home cooking. But he soon confined those longings to memory. This was his future—where he belonged.

Three weeks went by. Garett's face was never off the TV screen and the front pages of the newspapers. The novelty of a billionaire strolling back into work after disappearing like a high-school drop-out fascinated everyone—everyone except Sienna, it seemed. Garett had almost expected her to call, and when he hadn't heard from her he'd felt an unfamiliar twist of disappointment. Renewed publicity about his wealth had brought conquests old and new flocking around him, but not Sienna. Now he was beginning to realise he had underestimated her. She was different. He knew that now. She had never once asked him directly for money. Quite the opposite, he thought—and realised that for the first time since he'd left Entroterra he was smiling. His expression broadened still further when he remembered what she *had* begged him for, on that final night. And how often…

He leaned back in his chair. That was another new sensation. Work no longer filled his every waking moment. Sienna had cured him of that, by showing him how bad things could be for a woman married to an obsessive man. Aldo di Imperia had worshipped money. Garett's own father had been a slave to the bottle. Determined to avoid that particular fate, Garett had been married to his work and it had ruined his life, he realised. But meeting Sienna had changed all that. It had given him a wider perspective. Now he could see how life should be.

Happiness did not rely on how much money you had.

It came from within. And the greatest happiness came with the sort of love he had never imagined could exist for him: pure and simple. Meeting Sienna had allowed him to make that connection. It completed the circuit. The final piece in the jigsaw of his life had dropped into place. How could he have been so blind for so long? All these years he had been searching in a haphazard quest for fulfilment. Nothing had come close to providing him with a solution, because finding Sienna had been the answer to all the emptiness he had been trying to fill for the past thirty years. He realised now what he had been searching for all this time. There had been a hole in his life—and Sienna fitted it perfectly.

Now all he had to do was find out how to make everything right for her.

Sienna tried to blot out the memory of Garett, but it was hopeless. Visions of him and the ghostly touch of his fingers taunted her at every turn. The way he had walked out on her was seared into her mind for ever—but so were thoughts of his kindness, his body, and the night of love they had shared.

It was beyond all sense.

And that was what made Garett so unforgettable. He had shown her just how good life could be, and she loved him for it.

She loved him. That was the unbelievable truth.

You can have everything you want. Just reach out. There are no limits…

The last words Garett had said to her haunted Sienna's every waking moment. His voice echoed through her daydreams. He had brought her so much: self-esteem, and a sense of purpose. And Sienna's villa had been awakened from years of neglect. Garett's expertise had brought it back to life and given her a home to be proud of. Now she could walk through its grand halls and high passageways, marvelling at the gleam of gold leaf and the sheen of polished marble.

The house had changed out of all recognition, and so had Sienna. She had been a mousy, downtrodden little thing when Garett had first blown into her life. Now she felt…different. If it hadn't been physically impossible, Sienna would have sworn she was several inches taller. She was certainly lighter. Lately, she had lost her appetite. Garett was the cause of that, too. Thoughts of him left no time in her life for picking treats from the larder. Now the waistband of her jeans seemed roomier, somehow. Losing him had changed her—both physically and mentally. She was no longer afraid to look anyone in the eye. Garett had started by teaching her that everyone had a right to make the best of their life. He had given her the confidence to believe it.

Then he'd pulled the rug out from under her feet by abandoning her.

The only way Sienna could cope was by telling herself the whole affair had been a one-sided holiday romance. She could only deal with it by trying to make a completely fresh start. Her mind was made up. But her heart was empty.

Imelda was the first casualty of her broken dreams. Sienna's stepmother was moved into one of the newly refurbished estate cottages, next to Ermanno and his wife. Her rage counted for nothing, because Sienna was determined. She was going to sell the villa, and that meant losing its sitting tenant. The sale went through almost immediately, much to Sienna's relief. She could not wait to get back to the little village house where she had been born. It was her intention to open it as a bakery again, following the age-old tradition of her family.

Putting the worries and heartbreak associated with Entroterra and its estate behind her should have been a tremendous relief, but Sienna could not appreciate it. On her last day as owner of the villa, she took a final walk around the beautiful old house. Strolling into any of the grand salons, the ballroom or the drawing room, she could dazzle every newly restored corner with the flick of a light switch—but her life remained dark. Garett had left her a bed of roses, but she was alone in it. The single person who had made all this possible was lost to her for ever. His monument was in the perfect plasterwork and glowing gold leaf, the clean lines and classic beauty of a house ready to be filled and loved, as it deserved.

Leaning over the banisters, she gazed down into the airy entrance hall. From this vantage point she only half heard a car draw up outside, but there was no doubt somebody had arrived. She heard the vehicle's door slam, and the rattle of keys. Checking her watch, she pinned on her practised smile. The new owner was early.

She started along the landing, and down the wide, sweeping staircase. Her steps were slower and slower and she tried to put off the evil moment when she became a stranger in her own house. The villa had felt like a prison when Aldo was alive, but now it was showing its true potential, and she realised she was quite attached to the old place. It was all thanks to Garett. The irony was, her change of heart had come too late.

At the exact moment her foot touched the marble tiles of the ground floor, the great oak doors of the villa swung open. Sienna made a tremendous effort to raise her head and smile. Then she stopped.

'Garett? What are you doing here?'

'I might well ask you the same thing.'

His tone of voice gave nothing away. His expression was hidden from her too, as he entered the building and closed the door behind him. Then he turned and leaned back against the thick wood of the door, holding up the huge iron key that he had used to get in. 'I was told I would have vacant possession of my new home.'

'*You're* the buyer? But how?'

'The same way anyone buys a house anywhere.' His dark eyes were as watchful as ever. 'I told my agents where I wanted to live, and they found me an ideal place a few miles beyond Genoa. Then, as my pen was hovering over the dotted line, I got news that Entroterra was up for sale. The money you got for the painting wasn't enough for you, I take it?'

'Memories made me sell. Not money,' Sienna replied, flexing the spine of steel he had discovered for her.

Garett's lips moved, but they did not make it as far as a smile. When he spoke again it was with slow deliberation.

'Good ones, I hope?'

She shook her head.

'That's my fault, I suppose?'

She did not deny it.

He was dressed immaculately, in a dark suit and tie, white shirt, and black shoes polished to such a high gloss they reflected the chandelier in stars. Sienna remembered the times she had stared at his feet in the past, too nervous to look him in the eye. Now she could trap his gaze. She had to rely on hearing the squeak of his leather soles against the tiles to tell her that he was uneasy. There was certainly no sign of it in his steady, level stare.

'Sienna, when I left you here, I never expected to come back—but I could not stop myself. I've been a fool for thirty years. All it took was a few weeks with you to show me how life should be. I thought I could shrug off the experience and go back refreshed, but basically the same. It didn't work. I need the peace and tranquillity of this place, and, more importantly, I've discovered that I can't live without you.' His gaze held hers.

Sienna did not say anything for some moments. Dealing with agents and Imelda and every other trouble that had been forced onto her had taken an enormous toll. Faced with his confession, it all became too much. For a few seconds she forgot everything he had taught her. Lowering her head, she shook it slowly.

'What do you want me to say?'

He took half a dozen steps towards her across the echoing hall.

'I might have been attracted to a mouse, Sienna, but I fell in love with a girl who has more spirit than that.'

'Love?' She sprang back to life. 'You took me to bed, then you abandoned me!'

Sienna watched his reaction to her accusation. He looked as honest and apologetic as she felt, but she still had to know for certain.

'How do I know you won't leave me again, Garett?'

'Because I've come back to marry you.'

In one movement he covered the distance that still separated them and silenced her cry of astonishment with a long, lingering kiss. He kissed her until she could barely remember her own name, much less why she had been angry with him.

'You are mine, and you have been the only woman for me since the moment I first set eyes on you in the market,' he breathed, his voice dark with seduction. 'Marry me. I need you—now and for ever.'

There should have been no argument left. Garett had made up his mind, so there was no more to be said. It was one of the things about him that Sienna had known from the start. But she had to be sure.

'I don't want to be hurt again, Garett.'

'You won't be. I promise you that.'

'But you left me,' she persisted. 'You walked off and abandoned me while I was asleep in bed.'

'That was nothing but my stupid pride. It took a lot to keep me heading back to New York. I let work suck me into its vortex again—but nothing was ever the same. It couldn't be. My heart was no longer in it, so my team has taken control of the business, and I'm determined to take a back seat. I told the Bradleys I was coming back for you, but Molly says you've shut them out. I'm sorry, Sienna.' He threw up his hands and let them fall to his sides. 'I should never have left you. No amount of words can put that right. So will you let my actions speak for me?' he said slowly, a cautious smile playing around his lips.

For seconds on end they were held in a universe made for two. Then her lips parted in a slow smile.

She nodded, and immediately he took her in his arms.

Their kiss became a slow exploration of their new relationship.

'I just can't help acting on impulse where you are concerned,' he murmured softly, as his kisses moved from her lips to her earlobe.

'I don't mind that at all,' Sienna breathed, safe again in the security of his arms. 'All that matters is that you will never leave me again.'

'You can be quite sure of that, my love,' he murmured, sipping another kiss.

EXPECTING!

She's sexy, successful and pregnant!

Relax and enjoy our fabulous series about couples whose passion results in pregnancies... sometimes unexpected!

Our next arrival will be in April 2008:

ACCIDENTALLY PREGNANT, CONVENIENTLY WED

by Sharon Kendrick

Book # 2718

Having been burned badly before, Fleur Stewart wants to stay away from Spanish billionaire Antonio Rochas. But Antonio is sexy, smoldering and doesn't intend to let Fleur go easily....

www.eHarlequin.com

HP12708

HARLEQUIN®

Mediterranean NIGHTS™

*Things are heating up
aboard Alexandra's Dream....*

Coming in March 2008

ISLAND HEAT

by

Sarah Mayberry

It's been eight years since Tory Sanderson found
out that Ben Cooper seduced her to win a bet...
and eight years since she got her revenge. Now
aboard *Alexandra's Dream* as a guest lecturer for
her cookbook, she is shocked to discover the
guest chef joining her is none other than Ben!
And when these two ex-lovers reunite, the heat
starts to climb...in and out of the kitchen!

*Available in March 2008
wherever books are sold.*

Silhouette®

Desire

NEW YORK TIMES BESTSELLING AUTHOR

DIANA PALMER

A brand-new Long, Tall Texans novel

IRON COWBOY

Available March 2008
wherever you buy books.

I ♥

HARLEQUIN® *Presents*

BROUGHT TO YOU BY FANS OF
HARLEQUIN PRESENTS.

We are its editors and authors
and biggest fans—and we'd
love to hear from YOU!

Subscribe today to our online blog at
www.iheartpresents.com

What do you look for in a guy?

Charisma. Sex appeal. Confidence.
A body to die for. Looks that stand out from
the crowd. Well, look no further—in this
brand-new collection, available in April, you've
just found six guys with all this, and more!
And now that they've met the women in these
novels, there's one thing on everyone's mind....

Nights of Passion

One night is never enough!

The guys know what they want and how they're going
to get it! Don't miss any of these hot stories where
spicy romance and sizzling passion are guaranteed!

Look for these fantastic April titles!

www.eHarlequin.com

HPP0408

HAPPY
Valentine's Day
from Harlequin and Silhouette!

Special Treat!

Since you love books
as much as we do, we
would like to give you a
special Valentine's Day treat
of romantic and heartwarming reads.

Go to
www.HarlequinSpecialTreat.com
to receive your free online reads from us to you!

Plus there's even more, including fun romance
facts, upcoming news, games, e-cards and more!

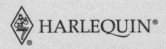 HARLEQUIN®

 *Silhouette*®

No purchase necessary.

VAL0208